*A Cold Springs Mystery*
*by*

# Sara Caudell

# Trail of
# Defects

A Cold Springs Mystery

By

*Sara Caudell*

# TRAIL OF

# DEFECTS

Dedication Page


This is dedicated to my family and
especially my husband without whose support I
would still be floundering in ink.

To my writing group, whose patience and
suggestions have made me a better writer.

# Cast of Characters

Kelly O'Conner – owner of Kelly's Bar
Arnold DuPree – Kelly's bouncer
Sheriff Jim Hobson – Sheriff of Cimarron Co.
Warren – part-time deputy
Randy – Deputy
Caroline Bristol Archer – Edna Bristol's daughter
Edna Bristol – Knee operation patient
Mark Archer- Caroline's husband
Joyce Hunter – Edna's cousin and care taker
Tiffany Hunter – daughter of Joyce.
Sarah Howard – physical therapist.
Mary Harris – nurse for Dr. Levine
Angie Hudson – runaway
Debbie Hudson – Angie's mother
Ross Campbell – Father of Vanessa Campbell-
Angie's friend
Travis Bristol – Edna's nephew
Mandy Bristol – Travis cousin, friend to Tiffany
Glen Hawkins – manager of Edna's hardware
store
Cliff – owner of the Wagon Wheel
Sally – tow truck driver.
Sharon Singleton – Public Defender

# CHAPTER 1

"See you tomorrow," Kelly O'Conner called to Arnold, his two-hundred forty pound bouncer, as he juggled the bank bag and keys to lock up Kelly's Lounge. The dim outside light above the door glowed through the darkness enough to show the outline of two trucks. They were parked in the dirt drive nestled between evergreen shrubs and an old shed.

The threatening rain clouds gave a slight chill to the air. It obscuring any light from the heavens and blackening the night sky. Ominously quiet and lacking the rustle of wildlife, the night sent a shiver down Kelly's spine. He shrugged it off. His day was not finished. He needed to make the bank deposit before he could head home. The peace and quiet of his warm bed enticed him. It had been a busy night, and he was bone-tired.

"Do I need to be here early tomorrow?" Arnold pushed his bulk behind the steering wheel of his white Toyota pickup and held the door open, listening for a response.

"No, I'll take care of the delivery tomorrow. Go home. Get a good night's sleep." Kelly waved him to leave, not wanting to impose on his employee's free time.

Arnold nodded, closed his pickup door

and drove around the building and across the gravel lot to the county road. Kelly walked around the side of the building barely able to make out the silhouette of the old planked-woodshed. He checked the door handle and made sure it was unlocked. His distributor's deliveryman picked up the empty beer kegs and left the full ones in the morning. Stuck back off the main county road, Kelly didn't worry about theft. The shed contained little of value, just a few restaurant supplies. Antique beer signs he couldn't part with were stored there, a couple of old wooden chairs, odds-and-ends of dishware, and two giant boxes of napkins. Nothing of value for anyone to steal.

Kelly was walking to his truck when he sensed someone behind him. It was not much, a flicker of movement and a tiny jolt of adrenaline. He started to turn around but felt the barrel of a gun pressed in the middle of his back. Kelly froze. A gloved hand came around reaching for the bank bag containing the bar's cash receipts. Quickly, his head buzzed with thoughts. He had been busy, and he had not made it to the bank as planned. This would cover his next mortgage payment. Kelly instinctively tightened his grip on the bag.

"Gimme," a low voice behind him growled, bumping the gun into his back.

Kelly hesitated, uncertain what to do when a bullet pierced the shed door. He released the bag. A hand pushed him against the shed. He caught himself before he fell. A sweatshirt-clad arm reached around him to open the door. Kelly turned his head in time to glimpse the sleeve of a dark hoodie and gun before he felt a thud. Pain echoed through his head. He fell into the shed. The door slammed shut behind him.

* * *

Cimarron County Deputy Randy Clark pulled up to Kelly's Lounge and checked the dash of his patrol car. The clock read three twenty-eight. He was in the south part of the county when he got the call that Kelly O'Conner had been robbed at gunpoint outside his bar. Clark, an ex-marine watched for movement in the dark parking area. He figured the robbery suspect to be long gone, but it paid to be alert and cautious. Both the bad guys and the good guys carried guns around here.

The old gray rough-wood structure had no windows in the front. The lonely florescent bulb in the parking lot cast a dim light over the front door. Three miles outside of the small mountain town of Cold Springs, Kelly's Lounge sat off a paved, potholed county road. The large parking lot pushed the building into the pine trees in back, lending the bar a picturesque feel. A wooden carport was against one side of the bar next to two small outbuildings.

The parking lot looked deserted. Randy remembered Kelly's employees always parked on the far side or in back.

He stepped out of the car, still uncertain if there were any lights on in the building. He walked over and banged on the door with the flashlight he had grabbed from his car.

He knocked a second time before he heard footsteps and locks clinking open and the door swung inward.

"It's about time!" The deep gruff voice of Arnold, Kelly's bouncer greeted the deputy. The six foot four man dressed in a black t-shirt and jeans stepped aside for the deputy to enter. Arnold, who would never reveal his ancestry, had worked for Kelly for the last six years. He kept his olive-brown head shaved but sported a long, black mustache that ended in a goatee. The ex-marine stood only five ten but was not intimidated by Arnold's size.

"Sorry, I was at the other end of the county. Was Kelly hurt? The dispatch didn't say." Randy entered the tavern as the lights went on, revealing the long wooden bar with stools on top, their legs reaching for the ceiling so the floor could be mopped. An odd assortment of wooden tables and mismatched chairs were scattered around the room. The odor of stale beer and cigarette smoke permeated the walls.

"A bump on the head and a few bruises.

Come on back." Arnold led the way between the two pool tables and into the back room Kelly used for storage and an office.

Kelly leaned back in his office chair holding an ice bag to the side of his head. "'Bout time you got here."

Fifty-year-old Kelly was stout with gray streaking his dark brown hair. He always wore a half smile.

"Yeah, I know. What happened, Kelly?" Randy took a notepad and pen out of his jacket.

"We closed up. Arnold got in his truck and pulled onto the road. I was over by the shed. I got my keys out to get in my pickup when this guy stuck a gun in my back and tried to grab the bank bag. I didn't turn around. I held on to the bag. When I wouldn't give it up, he put a bullet in the shed door. I handed the deposit over to him. He pushed me over to the supply shed and shoved me in, locked the door and took off." Kelly picked up the bottle of Advil from his desk, shook out two, and washed them down with a swallow of Laughing Lab beer.

There were only two chairs in the office, Arnold slid into the lone wooden seat across from Kelly and explained. "I was driving down the road and this car passed me going too fast on a mountain road. I slowed down and waited, I didn't see Kelly leave and remembered he needed to make the night deposit in town. So, I pulled off the road and waited a few minutes.

When he didn't pass me, I drove back. As I got out of my truck, I heard pounding coming from the shed."

Addressing Kelly, Randy asked, "Can you describe the guy?"

"Only a glimpse. He was shorter than I am. Smaller than I am. He wore a dark hoodie and maybe something over his face. A cloth of some kind or a scarf? I couldn't tell. When he hit me on the head, it wasn't much of a blow, but enough to knock me off balance and into the shed. I stumbled and fell inside. I didn't pass out. I heard a car start up and pull out. I guess they parked on the other side of the bar."

It was dark outside with no moon, but Randy still needed to ask, "I don't suppose you got a good look at the car?"

"Dark, small car." Arnold gave a shrug, unconsciously exercising his gloved right hand.

"Do you make deposits every night after you close?"

"No. Only Wednesday, Friday, and Sunday."

"Who knows about this schedule?"

"Most of my employees. A few regular customers."

"You mentioned he put a bullet in the shed door?"

Kelly nodded.

"Tell me about the shed. Was it locked? How did he unlock it and push you in?" Clark knew that sometimes people forgot to lock things up in the country but that was not the practice of most business people.

Putting the ice pack back on his head, Kelly frowned. "The shed wasn't locked. I leave the shed open on Friday nights with the empty beer kegs inside. My distributor comes here around eight o'clock on Saturday morning. I'm too tired from the night before to be here to meet him. He picks up the empty kegs and leaves my order in the shed and locks it up for me."

Randy considered this. The odds of this robbery being a stroke of luck for the thief were very slim. "Someone is aware of your habits. Any idea who might want to rob you?"

Glancing at Arnold, Kelly replied. "We were talking about it before you got here. We couldn't come up with a man with a slight build and a small car. A couple of guys who come in here probably thought they might try their hand at robbery but they both drive pickups and one of them is taller than I am."

"Can you tell me anything about the gun?"

"I caught a glimpse when he hit me, it was a black handgun. I don't have much knowledge of guns. Only how to use the shotgun I keep in the office." Kelly gestured towards a hefty black cabinet where he stored it. Then with a shake of the head and a sigh, "I'm hiring an electrician tomorrow to install better lighting in the parking lot." He glanced at Arnold who nodded in agreement.

"How much money did they take?"

Kelly pushed a copy of the deposit slip across the desk to Randy. "You can take that copy."

Seeing the large amount on the slip, he whistled. "You do this much business in what? Two days?"

Regret bemoaned Kelly's explanation. "I didn't make it to the bank Wednesday. That is what we took in in five days. Friday nights are usually busy. People stop by after work."

"Okay, come in tomorrow and sign the statement. It should be ready by noon. We'll talk about it again then. How is the head?"

"My wallet hurts worse."

"Let's go check out the bullet in the shed." The deputy motioned for Kelly to lead the way.

It took them a few minutes to find the bullet. It went through the shed door, hit one of the empty beer kegs and ricocheted, ending up in a commercial box of napkins.

"Well, it's a little banged up, but here it is." The deputy rummaged through the napkins and held up a small piece of metal. "This will be helpful when we find the guy who did this."

Stepping out of the shed so Kelly could close the door, Clark reminded the men, "I'll expect you to come by the office tomorrow."

# CHAPTER 2

"Get out! Just get the hell out of here!" Joyce Hunter, a hefty, stuffed-into-her-clothes fortyish woman, started toward Sarah Howard with fists clenched. Sarah didn't doubt that this woman was physically capable and had the conviction to throw her out. Joyce pushed past Sarah and opened the solid back door. Holding it open with white-knuckled, red-faced anger, she glared at Sarah.

Twenty-seven year old Sarah grabbed her shoulder purse and folders from the kitchen table and was turning to leave when she noticed Edna Bristol hanging onto her walker in the hall doorway. Her lips were trembling and tears were forming in the woman's tired green eyes. Joyce turned around to the elderly woman.

"Quit your blubbering and go back in your room," she bellowed. Edna shuffled back down the hall.

Turning on Sarah, Joyce jabbed a finger at her. "Now, see what you've done. She's going to blubber all afternoon now. Get out! And don't come back! You are not helping a damn thing here." She slammed the door as Sarah stepped onto the porch.

Sarah felt the door shutting as a bang of vibration on her back, the noise ringing in her ears.

"Well, now what do I do?" Sarah mumbled to herself as she stared at the closed door before going down the concrete steps and sidewalk to her car. Sarah sat for a few minutes staring at the white Rambler style house still trying to come to terms with being told to leave. She shook her head in disbelief and backed her Honda out of the driveway onto the street.

The dashboard clock read 1:25. Since her rehab at Edna's was cut short, she had time for coffee before her next appointment.

Her hands had finally quit shaking. The drama earlier rattled her more than she liked to admit.

She pulled into a parking spot in front of the Wagon Wheel Restaurant and Bar, one of the two eating places in Cold Springs. She straightened her green scrubs and fluffed her brown hair, thinking if she looked better, she would feel better. Opening the door of her Honda she got out, stepped across the sidewalk and opened the heavy wooden door.

Except for the neon Budweiser signs, the bar reminded her of a Hollywood western saloon set. The Wagon Wheel dated back to 1882 and little had changed since then. Lemon oil and cleaner masked the odor of stale beer that had seeped into the wood years ago. A massive ornately framed mirror behind the bar was still impressive for its size. It ran from bar level to the ceiling and the full length of the dark cherry wood bar that lined three-quarters of the width of the room. The bar was well maintained, the brass was worn off the foot rails but they were still shiny. Pictures of horses, cattle, and rodeos hung beside beer signs on the paneled walls. The old polished, wooden floor along with the glasses and bottles behind the bar sparkled in the overhead lights. Dark wood and burgundy leather booths lined two walls, tables and chairs filled the floor between them and the bar. The restrooms and kitchen were in the back. Along the side stood a raised platform for a band.

Ranchers and merchants lined up in front of the cash register to pay so Sarah nodded to the waitress and slid into the first empty booth.

Joyce Hunter made her lose her temper but the whole incident had upset her deep down. Something was terribly wrong at Edna's. Sarah worked as a physical therapist for seven years and she never had such a confrontation with a caregiver. *I came on too strong. Maybe the way I approached her was too critical. I was only trying to remind her what her responsibilities were to Edna. I don't like Joyce or how she's treating my patient.* She was trying to decide if her concerns had a valid foundation or if her personal dislike for Joyce was coloring the facts.

Sarah didn't think being thrown out of a house by a caregiver was the same as being fired. Especially since Joyce, the woman who did the throwing was not the one who hired her. *This is Friday. Do I show up Monday like nothing happened? What if she throws me out again or won't even let me in? Should I apologize? For what? For reminding her how to do her job and take better care of Edna?*

When the waitress finished collecting money, she set a glass of water in front of Sarah. "You're deep in thought. What's the problem, Sarah?"

Sarah smiled up at the waitress and sighed. "I just got thrown out of a patient's house."

"Edna Bristol's?"

This stunned Sarah. "How did you know?"

"I guessed. Connie Maxwell came in here yesterday complaining about Edna's caretaker not letting her visit her. She ran Connie off, too. What can I get you?"

"I'll take coffee. Oh, wait. Did the cook bake coconut cream pie today?" She limited her sweets but considering what happened, she decided to treat herself.

"One piece left," the waitress went behind the counter.

"I'll take it."

The waitress put down the silverware, the coffee and a plate with a towering slice of fluffy coconut pie.

"Thank you." Sarah picked up the coffee

the waitress set in front of her and realized that she was still shaky from her confrontation with Joyce.

Sarah thought about what the young lady told her. *I'm not the only one Joyce has a problem with. Is Joyce running all of Edna's friends off, too?*

It was a disturbing thought.

\* \* \*

Sarah had moved to Cold Springs a year ago to escape her abusive husband. She now worked in the rehab area of the local hospital two days a week. The other three days she made house calls to patients like Edna, who was recuperating from surgery. Sarah loved making house calls because it got her out of the clinic and into the beautiful Sawatch Mountain range of Colorado. She especially liked it during the spring and summer. Negotiating the roads in winter was more of a challenge when the snow piled up to be several feet deep and the nights were long.

Sarah took over sixty year old Mrs. Bristol's therapy from Becca when she took maternity leave. This was her third visit to her patient. She thought back on her first two visits. On her arrival Monday, she introduced herself and Joyce was polite but not really friendly as she ushered her to Edna's bedroom. Sarah introduced herself to her new patient and explained about Becca being on leave. Because her patient had taken her pain pills only minutes before the therapist arrived, Sarah was not able to start therapy until the pill took effect. They used this time to visit and become acquainted. Everyone seemed in good spirits when she left. Joyce didn't warm up to her, but neither was there any confrontation.

She recalled the Wednesday therapy session when Edna was clearly in pain as Sarah flexed her leg.

"I'm sorry this hurts. Did Joyce give you your pain pill before I came?" Sarah gently moved Edna's left leg up to bend the knee.

Mrs. Bristol was a small woman, flat on her back after knee replacement surgery. She avoided having the surgery until she fell on the icy steps four months ago. Now she was six weeks out of the hospital undergoing rehab.

Edna had lived at the end of Pike Street in Cold Springs ever since she married her high school sweetheart and moved into town. Five years ago, she had lost her husband of forty years. When her husband died, Edna leased out their hardware store and retired. She was alone except for a daughter living in Washington State and a son in the military.

The woman grimaced in pain and whispered, "We kind of both forgot you were coming today. Joyce gave me the pill as she saw you drive up."

Resting her leg back down on the bed, Sarah gave it a friendly pat. "Okay, I can wait for a few minutes before we start, but you need to remember. The sessions are only an hour each time and we need every minute to start those muscles moving, so you can walk again."

Sarah moved a chair closer to Mrs. Bristol's bed, pulled a form from her briefcase and sat down to ask about her general health. Sarah's usual routine was to start immediately massaging and stretching Edna's injured leg and exercising the good leg. Then, she would give her a break while she took her temperature, blood pressure, and oxygen level before she filled out the doctor's form.

"First question. Are you eating well?"

"Well. Ah, yes," Edna mumbled.

"You sound hesitant. Are you eating three meals a day? Do you finish your meals?" Some older patients became depressed after surgery. Sarah wanted to know if there was a problem she needed to report to the doctor.

"She feeds me what she likes and eats." She motioned with her head towards the kitchen where they heard Joyce making coffee.

"Joyce doesn't make the meals you like, so you don't eat much? Is that what you are telling me?" Sarah waited for an answer but Edna looked down at her hands clutching the sheets.

"What do you eat for breakfast?"

"Oatmeal."

"Does she put fruit and milk in the

oatmeal?" Sarah inquired.

"No."

"Just plain oatmeal?" The patient nodded her confirmation. "What about lunch? What do you eat for lunch?"

"Usually a peanut butter sandwich."

"That is all? A peanut butter sandwich?" She nodded.

Sarah sighed; she didn't like her patients' answers.

"What do you eat for dinner?"

"Joyce opens a can of soup."

Sarah made a note on the form. "Does she help you out of bed at least twice a day to sit in a chair with an ottoman?"

"Sometimes she forgets." She remembered the two times she tried to get up by herself. It caused excruciating pain. She had vomited on the bed and was afraid to tell Joyce.

"Do you remind her?"

"She remembers in the morning but in the afternoon, she doesn't like to be bothered when she's watching her programs," The woman whispered, knotting her fingers together.

"Her programs?"

"Game shows and soaps."

Sarah bit her tongue. "Okay. Let me take your vitals and then we will try moving that leg again." Sarah returned the chair to the corner and spotted the dust and lint balls attached to the chair leg. Joyce must not clean very often.

Another problem. I'll need to check Mrs. Bristol's bed sheets.

Joyce stepped into the bedroom. "I'm going to run to the drug store. I should be back before you leave." She was pulling on her sweater as she turned and rushed out the front door.

Sarah finished taking Edna's vitals and massaged her new knee. Before she started, "I need a drink of water. I'll be right back."

Entering the kitchen, Sarah took a glass down from the cabinet, turned on the water and peeked out the window to make sure Joyce's car had left. She then went to the refrigerator. Inside she found cheese, left over pork chops, a casserole, eggs, bacon, etc. Lack of food in the house was not why she fed Edna oatmeal and soup.

Sarah filled her glass with water and opened the cabinet by the stove. She counted nine cans of soup. Not much variety, chicken noodle, and bean. She took a sip of water and returned to her patient.

As she gently bent her leg, "Edna, when you first got home from the hospital your daughter was here with you, right?" Sarah remembered meeting her and her daughter in rehab. Her surgery was performed in a Denver hospital but she stayed at the small Cold Springs Rehab Center for a week afterward. Then Doctor Levine released her to go home.

"Yes, Caroline stayed here with me a week after I got home from the hospital. Then she had to go back to Seattle. She's married with two teenage boys. The boys both play sports, soccer, I think. Caroline sends me photos of them in their uniforms. They were all here last summer, the whole family." The elderly lady smiled. Her spirits and voice lifted as she talked about her family.

"You mentioned that Joyce is a relative?" Sarah had given both legs a massage and was now working to help her bend her new knee. The pain medicine had taken effect; she didn't flinch when Sarah worked her knee.

"Well, yes, a distant relative. Her uncle is married to my cousin. When my cousin found out I needed someone to stay with me she suggested Joyce. Joyce was out of work and needed a place to stay, so Caroline hired her."

"Do you talk to Caroline often?"

"She calls every other day and we talk for an hour or so. She always tells funny stories about the boys." Edna smiled, remembering her phone call last night.

"When Caroline was here, what did she fix you for breakfast?"

The patient let out a little yep of pain,

Sarah said, "I'm sorry, tell me if I am moving the knee too much."

"It's okay. I need to move it as much as possible. Well, when Caroline was here, she used to bring my breakfast in here and we would eat together. Usually, eggs and toast or sometimes she would fix waffles. I have an old waffle iron that still works. It browns them perfectly."

The noise of the front door opening stopped the conversation. They assumed Joyce had returned but a young, bleached-blond girl about twenty walked into the bedroom.

Agitated, with her hands on her hips she demanded, "Where's Mom?"

This confrontational girl surprised Sarah and embarrassed her patient. Edna stared at the floor, "She went out, Tiffany, I think to the drug store."

"Did she say when she would be back? I need to talk to her," the blond demanded.

"I don't think she gave a time. She only mentioned that she would be back before I left. The hour is up and I need to leave so I would expect her any minute now," Sarah answered sensing Edna didn't want to talk to her.

With a flip of her head, Tiffany abruptly turned and left the room. "I'll be in the den watching TV," she called back over her shoulder.

"I assume that is Joyce's daughter?" Sarah bent over so only Mrs. Bristol could hear.

"Yes, that's Tiffany," her patient growled. "She's supposed to be working in Gunnison. I bet she lost that job, too. The poor girl never learned how to get along with people. She doesn't like to work with the public but those are the only jobs she can find. Tiffany spends most of her time here watching television, fighting with her mother or hiding out in her bedroom."

Seeing how the girl made herself at home, Sarah wandered, "Does she live here, too?"

"Only when she's unemployed. She lost her last job a couple of weeks ago and Joyce made her find another. Tiffany used to clerk in a grocery store. I think she went to work at a convenience store this time. She found a friend here in Cold Springs who owns horses, and all she wants to do is hang out with her and ride."

"Well, since there's someone here with you, I need to leave. I have other patients to see. You need to remind Joyce to help you out of bed twice a day and talk to her about what you would like to eat. I'm sure she will fix it for you." Sarah felt sure Joyce was paid well for her services and Mrs. Bristol needed to assert herself more.

Sarah stepped into the den, "Tiffany, would you remind your mother that Edna needs her pain pill about 12:30 so when I arrive at 1:00 we can work for the entire hour. Also, she should be helped out of bed at least twice a day. The more she exercises her good leg the better headway we can make with the new knee."

Without turning to Sarah, Tiffany

grunted. Sarah took that for an answer and hoped it was positive. As she left, Sarah watched for Joyce's car hoping to spot it and go back to talk to her. No other cars passed her so she continued on her rounds.

Sarah parked her car in front of her next rehab patient's house and was sitting there trying to decide what she should do about Edna's eating. She would bring it up with Joyce on her next visit.

The therapist worried that something was seriously wrong at Edna's house. She would put at least the eating problem and her staying in bed into her weekly report to Doctor Levine. She would hold off telling about the pills. She knew it was easy to forget. Becca had gone over all the patient charts with Sarah but hadn't mentioned any problems. Maybe these problems would straighten themselves out if Mrs. Bristol asserted herself. She hoped so; otherwise, she would report them to both Doctor Levine and the Sheriff. Colorado had recently passed a law about reporting possible abuse of the elderly. Sarah felt Edna's situation might fall into that category. She had never had to report anyone before.

* * *

Friday came and Sarah found herself on the front steps of the 1950's, blue-trimmed, white ranch house. Tiffany opened the door, saw Sarah and hollered back over her shoulder, "Yeah, Mom, it's her." Leaving the door open Tiffany returned to flop on the couch in the den. Sarah entered the house carrying a walker and went down the hall to her patient's room. "Good morning."

Edna sat in a chair beside her bed with a bowl of cold oatmeal on the nightstand. She turned, smiled at Sarah and took hold of the chair arms and rose from the chair. "I can almost get in and out of the chair by myself. My new knee doesn't bend well yet but if I'm careful it doesn't hurt too bad." The pride of accomplishment showed in her smile.

"Good, I brought you a walker and I'll show you how to use it. Now, let's put you back in bed and go through our exercises." Sarah helped her back in bed and massaged her legs.

"Did you eat your breakfast?"

Looking at the bowl on her nightstand, she shook her head.

"Did you ask Joyce to fix you eggs or something else?" Again shook her head. Sarah let out a long sigh.

"Have you had your pain pill?" Edna flinched as Sarah moved her leg.

"Yes. When she helped me into the chair a few minutes ago." She didn't mention she was trying to get out of bed by herself when Joyce brought her pill and helped her sit in the chair.

"Okay, until the pain pill takes effect, why don't I show you how to use the walker?" Sarah helped her patient out of bed and into the walker. "Now, don't put weight on the new knee, just scoot the walker and use the good leg. Keep most of your weight on your arms as you lift your good leg." She did as she was told. "That is great, one tiny step at a time."

Sarah couldn't concentrate on the therapy. Her mind kept wondering back to the problems with Joyce. After a few minutes, "Okay, why don't you sit in the chair for a few minutes and rest?" Sarah helped her patient into the chair by the bed.

"Edna, I'll be right back." Sarah went to the kitchen where the women were talking. It sounded like Tiffany was asking Joyce for money and she was given a flat 'no'. Sarah worried that Joyce was not in a good mood but she needed to speak to her.

"Joyce, could I talk to you a second?" Sarah smiled at Tiffany and her mother at the table.

"I guess." Joyce's words gave grudging permission.

"Edna needs her pain pill at least thirty minutes before I arrive at one. She needs to be up and out of bed for several hours a day and if possible helped to stand and take a step or two. I brought her a walker, and it's important that she use it and walk around as much as possible."

"Yeah, you keep telling me that stuff. That old woman doesn't cooperate. Look, it's hard enough for me to take her back and forth to the bathroom all time. She's always complaining about how her leg hurts every time she moves. She complains about her meals. I'm tired of her damn complaining all time."

"Okay, I understand how a person with limited mobility would be irritable. It happens with a lot of older people. They aren't used to having to depend on someone else for the things they used to do on their own. But it is important that she's given her medication on time and is helped to get around as much as possible. The more she's up and about the faster her healing time." Sarah tried to be sympathetic but insistent. "I think if you both try a little harder and are a little more patient, her recovery will go faster."

"You think that, do you? Well, you try putting up with her hollering all time needing to go to the bathroom. Needing her pills. Needing another blanket. I didn't take this job to be her slave or her servant." Joyce raised her voice and stood. Sarah noticed Tiffany edge towards the doorway to escape the room.

"No, but you were hired to take care of her and you knew she just had knee surgery. I'm sure her daughter is paying you well." Sarah realized the conversation was escalating but couldn't stop it. This woman was not taking care of her patient and she was now showing how out of control the situation was becoming. Sarah stood with her mouth open staring as Joyce continued her rant.

"Not well enough to change her bed when she pees in it. Not well enough to get up in the middle of the night when her 'tummy aches'. I'm tired of you and that other woman telling me what I'm supposed to be doing. I'm damn tired of it so why don't you leave."

"I'm sorry Joyce, maybe I came on too strong. I'm sure we can come to some arrangement."

Joyce slammed her fist on the table. "Get out! Just get the hell out of here!"

\* \* \*

Now what? Now, what do I do? I guess I'm obligated to tell Doctor Levine.

Sarah checked her watch and realized she needed to visit her next patient. She had time to plan exactly what she would tell the doctor.

When she finished making her house calls, Sarah stopped at the small state-of-the-art Mountain View Hospital that served Cimarron County. It was only about four years old and took care of emergencies, birthing, minor surgery, and rehab. Anything else was transported to Denver or Colorado Springs by ambulance or helicopter. It was a two-story, glass and brick building with a parking lot in front. The backdrop for the structure was the evergreen-covered Sawatch Mountain Range.

Sarah knocked on Doctor Levine's office door at the medical center and waited for a response.

"Come in, if you're bringing coffee with you," came the bellow from the other side of the door, the doctor's usual response.

She opened the door, coffee in hand. "Do you have a few minutes Doctor Levine?"

"For you, Sarah, anytime." The head of the Mountain View Community Hospital said, taking the coffee and setting it on his desk. The sixty-year-old, slender physician had on his hospital issued white jacket. His horn-rimmed glasses sat perched on his nose below the bushy gray eyebrows. Seeing her worried look, he motioned for her to take a seat in one of the visitor's chairs, "Now, I'm feeling this is not a social visit."

"No, I'm afraid not. It's about Mrs. Bristol."

"That is surprising. I found Edna to be very pleasant and her knee surgery went well."

"Yes. Well. Her daughter hired a lady to take care of her, a relative. When I go over for her rehab, she hasn't been given her pain pill or, if she ha, it was as I drove up. The caregiver doesn't help her out of bed like she should." Sarah told the doctor the rest of the problems.

"And the caregiver and I had a confrontation, and she told me to leave and not come back."

"Well, that sounds like several problems. Let's take them one at a time. You've met her daughter. Right?"

"Only to be introduced. I took over from Becca when she went on maternity leave."

"Okay. How is Edna's progress?"

"From what I can tell from Becca's first reports and what I have seen, she's not much better than before she left the hospital."

"That is not good. When is your next visit?"

"Supposed to be next Monday."

"Hold on a second." Doctor Levine picked up the phone and punched in two numbers. "Mary, are you busy? Can you come to my office? Thanks." Turning back to Sarah, "Mary Harris will be here in a minute. I'll check if she can go over with you on Monday. Another opinion would be welcome."

A quick knock on the door and Mary stuck her head around the corner. "What can I help you with?"

Mary Harris, a Physician's Assistant, had been a nurse in Cold Springs for twenty years before she went back to college and got certified. She was born and raised in Cimarron County and knew everyone there and how they were related to each other. Like a lot of middle-aged women, she had gained weight over the years but it didn't slow her down. She could run up and down the hospital halls with the best of them.

Doctor Levine motioned Mary inside. Sarah and the doctor explained the problems Sarah was having at the Bristol residence.

"Edna isn't eating well because Joyce isn't fixing her meals. Joyce doesn't help her out of bed or remember to give her the pain pills. The house isn't being cleaned. You've known the Bristol family for a while. What do you think?" the doctor pointed the question at Mary.

Sarah interrupted, deciding she had to tell her suspicions along with the facts. "One other thing. I worry there may be some mental abuse going on, too. I have no idea how bad it is, but she acts afraid of Joyce. There are no signs of physical abuse. She acts like she's afraid to say anything that might make the woman angry. Also, the woman may be taking her things. I saw Joyce's daughter wearing Edna's new sweater."

Folding her arms across her middle, Mary injected her opinion, "Someone needs to call Caroline, Edna's daughter and tell her what is going on. She only has Caroline and a son but the son is in the military. I remember something about him being stationed overseas. I can assure you that Caroline would never put up with this kind of treatment of her mother. I've never heard of this Joyce. Edna's sister died a few years ago but I'm sure she still has relatives over by Colorado Springs."

Mary glanced between the doctor and Sarah then sighed and asked what they were both waiting to hear. "Do you want me to call Caroline and tell her the problems?" With that, both the doctor and Sarah let out the breaths they were holding and smiled.

"I would rather you did. I hate to introduce myself by telling a client's daughter I was thrown out of their house." Sarah was still embarrassed about that.

"Mary, you are acquainted with Edna and Caroline best. I think the call would have more credence coming from you." Doctor Levine smiled.

"Do you have Caroline's number?" The doctor pushed the patient's file across the desk to Mary.

Sarah smiled at the two, relieved at how this was resolving. "Thank you so much. I need to go home." She closed the door behind her.

Mary sat for a few minutes staring at the physician, wondering if his thoughts were along the same lines as hers. "Doctor Levine, do you think this woman could physically hurt Edna?"

"I don't know. It crossed my mind." He hesitated then finished. "Mary, we don't have much information about this woman, let's not jump to any conclusions; Sarah didn't notice any signs of physical abuse, after all."

# CHAPTER 3

Late Saturday evening, Sheriff Jim Hobson and Deputy Warren Carpenter pulled the cruiser in behind the emergency medical vehicle blocking the driveway of the Cottonwood Inn Bed and Breakfast. The call came in minutes ago from the owner of the inn, Margaret Anderson. She found a woman's body in the parking lot when she returned from bingo at the VFW Hall.

The law officers exited the police car and walked past the EMS vehicle. Two emergency techs were bent over a dark-haired woman in her forties. She lay on the asphalt beside an open car door, bleeding from a chest wound. Warren walked around to the back of the late-modeled Honda. He noticed the license plates had a rental car sticker beside it. He then reached inside the passenger door and picked up the purse lying on the floor.

Coming around the car with a woman's wallet in his hand, "Washington State license, Caroline Archer, age forty-two. This is a rental car. About eighty dollars in cash and several credit cards. My guess is that it wasn't a robbery unless she had something else of value. The keys are still in the ignition."

Jim Hobson, the fifty-year-old Sheriff of Cimarron County, watched the young emergency tech hoping for a positive outcome. The tech shook his head slightly, alerting the officer of her death. The techs carefully backed away leaving their equipment.

"Warren, call Doctor Levine and Randy, tell them we have a body. Keep everyone else away." The Sheriff studied the street where a few trucks and cars were stopping, drawn by the flashing emergency lights.

Warren, a tall, muscular rancher and part-time deputy returned to the cruiser, radioed dispatch for Randy Clark and the doctor. He took out the yellow crime scene tape and closed off the area. Signaling the audience to continue on down the road, he allowed the EMS techs to cross the tape and walk back into their vehicle.

After talking to the Sheriff and filling out the forms, the techs waited in their vehicle. Warren put on his plastic gloves and booties, got out his camera and snapped photos of the crime scene, starting out by the tape and working towards the body. He finished up as Clark arrived with a floodlight and other crime scene equipment. Both men grabbed flashlights and started to meticulously examining the area around the car.

Sheriff Hobson noticed Margaret waiting for him on the front steps of her bed and breakfast. The Cottonwood Inn was an old three-story Victorian house with a wrap-around porch and balcony. It had enough gingerbread accents to keep a painter busy all year round. Margaret had her arms crossed in a self-hug.

"Margaret, how are you doing?" He approached the pale, shaken woman.

"Well, Jim, I've certainly been better." She regarded the bloody scarf she had dropped by her feet. It used to match the blue and white paisley blouse she wore. "I tried to stop the bleeding. But there was just so much blood."

Margaret, a sixty-year-old, gray-haired grandmother opened her old Victorian house as a bed-and-breakfast five years ago to supplement her retirement.

"Margaret, I'm sure you did all you could. Can you tell me what happened?"

Taking a deep breath, "I had gone to bingo at the Hall, but I got a headache and came home early. When I pulled into the driveway, I saw that car parked there with the door open. I thought I had a customer. I pulled around to the side of the building where I always park and walked around to the front. That is when I saw her lying on the ground. I ran over. The woman was lying there bleeding. I took off my neck scarf and pressed it on the wound. I called 911 on my cell and waited. It only took a few minutes before they arrived."

"Did you see anyone or anything before you drove up beside the car? Was anyone pulling out of the parking area when you went to turn in?" Sheriff Hobson with paper and pencil in hand took notes.

"No, I didn't notice another car." Margaret hesitated as she tried to recall exactly. "I don't remember anyone walking by either." Seconds later, she added, "The neighbor's dog was barking. Mr. Larson called him inside as I drove in."

"You don't happen to know the woman, do you? Her driver's license says she's Caroline Archer."

Margaret gasped. "Oh my goodness, I didn't recognize her. Jim, that is Edna Bristol's daughter! She must have been coming home to visit her mother again. Edna had knee surgery several weeks ago. I haven't seen Caroline to talk to her in several years."

"I am acquainted with Edna. I vaguely remember her daughter. Was she staying here at your bed-and-breakfast?"

"No, I don't have any guests for tonight. That is why I went to bingo."

"What can you tell me about the daughter?"

"She went to college in Greeley, met and married her husband there. They lived in Denver for a few years then moved to Washington State. I think Seattle. I'm not sure. She has two boys. I don't remember what her husband does for a living. Caroline comes down several times a year to visit her mother. That is pretty much all I can tell you."

"Thanks, Margaret." Hobson noted the lights still on at the Larson's house next door so decided he would talk to Don before he went to bed.

Rounding the hedge, he walked up the sidewalk to the front door. The door opened before he could knock and Don, a small man in his fifties, stood in the doorway. "I figured I'd be your next stop, Sheriff."

He held out his hand to the old resident, "Don, you didn't happen to see the shooting did you?"

Don shook his hand and stepped back for him to enter the living room.

"No, but I guess Molly and I both heard the shot." He petted the cocker spaniel's head. "There was a bang when I was in the kitchen. Molly was outside barking, but by the time I got to the front porch, there wasn't much to see. Of course with that hedge, I can only see part of Margret's parking lot. I saw her pass my house and pull into her drive a few minutes later."

"You didn't see or hear anyone running or anything like that?"

"No running, but I heard a car leave from a couple of houses down, didn't see it of course with so many trees in the way. It was a dark blob heading south on Aspen. Who got shot?"

"I can't tell you who right now, Don. However, I can tell you they didn't make it." Don slowly shook his head in silence.

"Anything else?"

"No, sorry."

"Thanks, Don. If you think of anything else, give me a call." Hobson left through the front door and returned to the parking lot. He checked if Warren or Randy had found anything and if Doctor Levine had arrived.

Doctor Levine stood after squatting down by the body. "Evening, Jim. You know who this is?"

"Margaret recognized the name. Edna Bristol's daughter."

Doctor Levine froze. "This is Caroline Archer?" He gave a slow headshake, "I was expecting her in the next few days, but not like this. If you are through with the body, I'll have EMS transport her to the morgue. I need to return to the hospital, there is a nine-year-old waiting for stitches. I have information that might be of value on Mrs. Archer. It's kind of complicated, so I'll be over in the morning to talk to you."

Looking at his deputies, who were now standing by the doctor, the Sheriff asked, "Are you through with the body?"

The deputies both nodded. Warren added, "We have the photos, fingerprints off the car door and very little else. No footprints or tire marks on this asphalt. Looks like she stepped out of her car and someone shot her."

"Don said he heard a car pull out a few

houses down and headed south on Aspen. You might be able to find something."

The deputies left with flashlights in hand. The techs came with the gurney, put Caroline in a body bag and left. Hobson took his own flashlight and went over the crime scene. He didn't figure he would find anything since Warren and Randy hadn't but it was a habit with him. He needed to picture the entire crime scene in his head and this was the best way for him to do it.

Searching through the deceased's purse that Warren put back on the front seat, the Sheriff found her husband's business card with a cell number. He called the police in Seattle and asked if they would inform Mr. Archer of his wife's death. The call back from the police came twenty minutes later informing him the Archer house was dark, and no one responded when the officers knocked on the door. He thanked them and checked his watch. It would only be eleven thirty in Washington so he punched in the husband's cell phone numbers.

"Hello," a man answered with a background noise of a car.

"Mr. Archer?"

"Yes."

"This is Jim Hobson, with the Cimarron County Sheriff's office in Cold Springs. Mr. Archer, are you driving a car?"

"Yyyes. Why?"

"Please pull off the road. I need to talk to you and I want your full attention."

"Okay, what's going on? I am off the road." Archer's voice got loud with confusion.

"There's been an accident. Mr. Archer, where are you?"

"I'm outside of town. Is it Edna?"

Hobson hated this kind of conversation. "No, sir. Are you the husband of Caroline Archer born 1-12-1977?"

"Yes. Yes, I am. That's Caroline's birth date. Has something happened? Is she hurt?" The husband's agitation grew.

"Mr. Archer, I have the unpleasant chore of informing you that your wife was shot. We found her in the parking lot of the Cottonwood Inn in Cold Springs. How soon can you be here?"

"Oh, god. No. Wait. Wait. I can't hear you," his voice broke up.

The Sheriff listened to him turn off his car engine and the connection became clearer. "You said my wife was shot. How is she? What hospital is she in?"

"I'm sorry, Mr. Archer your wife didn't make it to the hospital." The officer hated to break the news to the husband so abruptly but the connection was not clear and he needed him to understand.

"But . . . but, I talked to her." Confusion and disbelief echoed down the phone line.

"I'm sorry, Mr. Archer, we found her body about an hour ago. The EMS couldn't revive her. How close are you to Cold Springs?"

"Sheriff, I am not far from town. I should be there in about thirty minutes. I got a flight out of Seattle right after Caroline did. I was going to meet her at her mother's. She's dead," he murmured.

"Okay, do you know where the sheriff's office is? Do you know where the town square is?" He gave the husband directions to the county courthouse and his basement office; the back door would be unlocked.

Mr. Archer acknowledged the directions with a sobbing groan.

***

The small town of Cold Springs, Colorado, is a ranching community nestled between the rampart and the Sawatch Mountains covered with aspen, pine, fir, and, along the creek bed, cottonwoods. The population is about eighteen hundred people on a good day. Besides Cold Springs and a couple of other small towns, Grant County encompasses several large ranches and dozens of smaller ones. Most all are cow-calf operations handed down from generation to generation. The meadows and rolling hills, make it prime ranch land. It is off all the major highways and the ski resorts are to the north. They have a few tourists during the summer but for the most part, the town and surrounding area are left to the locals.

While Hobson waited for the husband to arrive, the deputies came in with what little evidence they had collected and stashed it in the locked evidence closet in the back. Randy would go back out to the scene after dawn and see if he could find anything they may have missed. Warren, the part-time deputy, went home and Randy got a call to help the highway patrol with a car off the road. They left, passing a confused-looking man in the hallway.

Mr. Archer wandered into the office and Hobson could tell that grief had set in. His shoulders slumped, his eyes were red, and he had a dazed look. The Sheriff took his arm and led him to a chair. "Can I get you anything? Water? Coffee?"

"Coffee, if you have it. I was in such a hurry, I didn't stop to eat." Then realizing he didn't remember the man's name, "Sorry, I'm Mark Archer."

Handing him a cup of sugared coffee, Hobson shook his hand and sat down beside him. "I'm Jim Hobson. I've known Edna Bristol for a long time. I can't say I remember Caroline as an adult. I do remember the little girl who used to sit by the cash register of the hardware store with her dad."

Mark gave a half smile. Taking a long drink of coffee, He spoke his mind. "We argued last night. About Edna, Caroline had just gotten back from here a few weeks ago and last night she insisted she had to come back. I didn't understand why she kept saying that her mother wasn't doing well. She wouldn't explain, only said that things weren't working out as planned. She was real upset. I decided to wait until morning and talk to her again but when I got ready for work, she had already left the house." He lifted his head and detected a question on the Sheriff's face. "Yes, I've been working Saturdays for the last couple of months. The boys said she had a suitcase with her and she was going to Grandma's. She would be back in a few days. I was on my way to work this morning when I decided I needed to go with her and help straighten out the problem. I tried calling her but I think her phone was turned off. I assumed she had already boarded the plane before I made my decision. I couldn't reach her to tell her I was coming, too." His voice broke off. "I called the neighbor lady to look after the boys 'til we got back."

Jim Hobson sat and listened. Caroline's husband was still processing the events. The Sheriff decided he needed to explain to this sorrow-stricken husband the circumstances of his wife's death. He needed Mark to answer questions as soon as possible.

"Mr. Archer, your wife was shot in the chest in the parking lot of a bed-and-breakfast here. We are conducting a murder investigation."

"Murder? You said she was shot. I thought it was some kind of freak accident. Why would someone want to shoot my Caroline? Was it a robbery? She doesn't carry much cash. She relies on credit cards." He slowly shook his head, his mind in a haze.

"Where are you staying tonight, Mr. Archer?"

"I was going out to Edna's . . . Oh, my god, did you tell her mother?"

Assessing how upset and confused the husband seemed, the Sheriff suggested, "Why don't you ride with me over to Edna's to tell her. You can come back and get your car tomorrow." Mrs. Bristol lived at the end of town, less than a mile from the Courthouse.

Leading him out to his squad car, "How long have you and Caroline been married?"

"We met in college. I finished my masters after Desert Storm, while Caroline was working on her bachelors degree. We were married after we graduated. We have two sons, sixteen and twelve. They are staying with a neighbor," Mark was trying to pull his life back together in his head. The Sheriff could tell Mark's mind was not completely registering that his wife was dead.

Mr. Archer had slumped into the car seat

with his head in his hands, "How am I going to tell the boys? How do you tell kids their mother is dead? Their world as they knew it had ended. Oh, god, no."

Getting on his car radio he called his dispatch, "Dee, would you call Doctor Levine and ask him to meet us at Edna Bristol's house? Thanks."

As they were pulling up to the Bristol house, the dispatcher came on the car radio, "Sheriff, Doctor Levine can't make it. He's sending Mary Harris."

"Okay, thanks."

He pulled the police cruiser into the driveway behind an older car then helped Mark out of the car. They walked up to the dark house and rang the doorbell. Moments later, the front light flipped on and a haggard looking woman in an old housecoat and bare feet opened the door.

"I'm Sheriff Hobson and this is Mark Archer, can we speak to Edna?" He motioned to the badge on his shirt.

"Why, what's going on? What do you want her for?" Her defensive, demanding attitude was apparent. She did not step away from the door to let them in.

"We need to inform her that her daughter's been killed." The Sheriff took hold of the door and gently pushed his way into the house. He didn't recognize this woman but instinctively disliked her. A glance at Mark with his mouth open and wide-open eyes confirmed his assessment of the woman.

"I assume Mrs. Bristol is in bed. Would you wake her and tell her Jim Hobson would like to speak to her?" He remained standing in the living room, arms crossed.

Joyce glared at him, then walked down the hall to Edna's room. The lawman watched the woman enter one of the bedrooms. Waiting to see Edna, the Sheriff answered the tap at the front door. Mary Harris stood on the front porch. "Thank you for coming, Mary. You heard what happened?"

Stepping inside she nodded, "They said Caroline was killed?"

"Yes, shot in the chest at the parking lot of the Cottonwood Inn," The Sheriff spoke softly.

Coming out of Edna's room, the woman grudgingly motioned for the men to go down the hall. "Well, she's awake." Then noticing Mary, she demanded, "Who is she?"

"I'm Mary Harris. I am a physician's assistant and an old friend of Edna's. And you are . . . ?" Mary made no move to be polite and shake the woman's hand.

"I'm Joyce, Edna's niece, I take care of her." She snapped and went to the kitchen.

Mrs. Bristol struggled to sit up in bed as the trio entered the room. Horror stricken, and shaking her head, "Jim, she said Caroline is dead? Oh, Mark. No, no that can't be right."

She held her arms out to her son-in-law. Mark put his arms around her and held her close. They cried together for a few minutes before Archer moved to the far side of the bed still holding on to Edna's hand. Hobson had wanted to break the news gently and didn't appreciate Joyce telling her before he could.

"I'm sorry, Edna, I wanted to tell you myself. We found Caroline in the parking lot of the Cottonwood Inn. She was shot in the chest. EMS couldn't revive her. She passed away about an hour ago." The Sheriff explained.

"I heard sirens . . . before I went to sleep. I knew she was coming to visit. She called last night. She said she missed me." She tried to talk between sobs, using the corner of a bed sheet to wipe the tears. Mary reached over and handed her the box of tissues from the dresser.

"How did . . . this happen? Was it . . . an accident? Who . . . would . . . hurt my baby?" Mrs. Bristol was having trouble getting her breath and was hiccupping between words. Mark was wiping away his tears with his sleeve. Mary put her arm around the woman and handed Mark tissues.

"We don't have much information. I don't think it was an accident. We'll find who did it." The Sheriff leaned over close to her face, "Edna, do you have any more questions for tonight? If not, I will be back in the morning. Mary will stay here as long as you need her."

He turned to Mark, "Do you want to stay here? I can take you to a motel if you would rather."

Wiping at his eyes, "I have some questions. I'll go with you." Then leaning down to the older woman, "If I don't see you later tonight, I'll be back in the morning."

"Oh, no! What about the boys? Have you told them yet?" Edna sobbed again and grabbed Mark's sleeve.

"No. That is what I am about to do." Mark whispered, patting her hand.

Mark dreaded the responsibility ahead of him. As the men walked from the bedroom, the Sheriff caught site of a shadow disappearing down the hall into another bedroom. Mary led them to the front door, let them out and locked it behind them.

Outside, Mark cleared his throat, "Sheriff, would you take me to the nearest motel? I need to call my sons. I don't want to use my cell and I would like to be alone."

He nodded his understanding. "There are two motels, one is better than the other. I suggest the Western Star. It's at the other end of town on Main Street. I'll take you to your car; if you feel well enough to drive?"

"That'll be fine." His head cleared with the cool night air. They got in the cruiser and returned to the sheriff's office.

When they got out of the car, he reminded Mark, "You need to come to my office in the morning. How does ten o'clock sound?"

"Fine, I'll be here. Good night."

# CHAPTER 4

Eight o'clock the next morning, Doctor Levine arrived at the hospital and met Sarah Howard leaning against the desk talking to the receptionist. Sarah wore jeans and a red sweatshirt. She had accessed the hospital's morning grapevine. As he approached, Sarah turned towards him with an expression of horror, "Doctor Levine, did you hear that Caroline, Edna's daughter was killed last night?"

"Yes, Sarah. They called me. Do you want to come to my office?" he motioned down the hall.

"What happened?" Sarah fell into step beside the physician.

After a quick stop in the break room, they went to the doctor's office. "Mrs. Anderson at the bed and breakfast found Caroline Archer in her parking lot dead from a gunshot wound. We need to talk to Jim Hobson and tell him everything about why she was here."

"You don't think it was a robbery? I realize this is a small town but we do have a few problems at times."

"No, her rings, watch and her purse were still on her body. So no, I doubt if the Sheriff thinks it's a robbery."

"Oh, my god, do you think her coming here got her killed? Do you . . . you think Joyce had something to do with it? Oh, no. Maybe we shouldn't have called her."

Doctor Levine sat in silence letting Sarah's mind sift through her thoughts.

"No, wait. Joyce would have just been fired that's all. No one kills for that." As soon as a thought popped into her head, it came out of her mouth. "I'm not even sure what was happening would be considered abuse. Really, only neglect. No, no. It must have been a robbery or possibly road rage? You hear of that sometimes." Her eyes appealed to Doctor Levine for his thoughts.

"I'm sure it's nothing to do with Edna but we need to tell the Sheriff what happened. It's his problem, not ours."

"Well, what do I do Monday? Should Mary and I still go out to Edna's?"

"We'll talk to the Sheriff. Do you have time now for us to go talk to him?"

"Sure, this is my day off."

Twenty minutes later Sarah and Doctor Levine entered the back door of the old, red stone Cimarron County Courthouse. Near the stairwell hung a wall directory listing all the county offices. Taped on the front of the directory was a homemade sign: "Court" with an arrow up and "Jail" with an arrow down. They went down the worn oak steps to the basement and found the old wooden door with banker's glass with "Sheriff's Office" stenciled in gold paint.

Jim Hobson stood in the reception area talking to Dee, the young dispatcher, when the couple walked in.

"Sheriff Hobson, do you know Sarah Howard? She's one of the physical therapists at the hospital. She visits Edna Bristol three days a week." Doctor Levin introduced the two.

"Nice to meet you, Sarah." Then looking at the physician, "Is this about Caroline Archer?"

"Yes, Jim. I think we have some information about what led up to Caroline coming back to Cold Springs."

Hobson led the way to his office and relaxed into his desk chair. "Please sit down Sarah. Take your time. I want all the details." He motioned to the chairs in front of his desk.

"Do you mind if I tape this?" He gazed from the doctor to Sarah.

The doctor nodded his head to Sarah, "I think that would be okay, don't you, Sarah?"

She agreed. Then making herself comfortable, Sarah related her last three visits to Edna's. Not wanting to overstate anything, Sarah carefully explained the dirty house; the diet Joyce had Edna on and the neglect of her patient's medical needs.

When Sarah finished, Hobson had a better understanding of why Mary Harris called Caroline Archer and why Caroline came back to Cold Springs. He turned off the recorder, "Thank you, Sarah. Doctor Levine,you did the right thing having Mary call Caroline. If you think of anything else, call me."

"Should I go out Monday for her physical therapy?" Sarah needed the Sheriff guidance.

"I would call first and talk to Edna or her son-in-law, Mr. Archer. Make sure she's up to rehab. Here is his cell phone number." Hobson grabbed one of his business cards off his desk and wrote Mark's cell number on it before handing it to Sarah.

She and the doctor left the office, and the Sheriff sat down at his desk and stared at his notes. After talking to Sarah he knew part of what was going on at Edna's. It explained the hostility of Edna's caregiver.

Now he needed information on the family from Seattle. He picked up the phone and called the homicide investigator for the city of Seattle. He called in a personal favor from a man he met at a training session at Quantico last year. Hobson paid his own way to the training but the information and the contacts were worth it.

"Jeff Sherman, please," he asked the operator then he listened to two clicks.

"Sherman," came a male voice a few seconds later.

"Jeff, this is Jim Hobson from Cold Springs, Colorado. I need a favor."

"I can be down there with my fishing pole day after tomorrow," Jeff quickly replied.

Jim laughed, "I would love to tell you that

an overstock of rainbow trout was my problem. But I need you to check up on a man and wife named Mark and Caroline Archer. Caroline was shot in a parking lot here last night. Mark showed up shortly afterward. Can you give me a couple of hours? Would you check with their neighbors and employers? I would appreciate it."

"Sure, I just finished up a case and I don't have to be in court until Wednesday. Besides, it will give me a chance to ignore the paper work on my desk for a few hours. I'll call you back soon."

After giving the detective Archer's address and other pertinent information, the Sheriff thanked Jeff.

Hobson headed to the break room for more coffee, and he realized it must be ten o'clock already because Mark Archer entered the reception area.

Within minutes they settled into the sheriff's private office for the interview. Hobson, sitting behind his old oak desk started with the questions. "Mr. Archer, last night you said something about having an argument with your wife?"

"Well, yes. It was the night before last." Mark hesitated. "My wife was killed. Am I a suspect? Should I ask for a lawyer?"

"Mr. Archer, I can't tell you if you need a lawyer or not. Right now I am trying to piece together the events that happened before your wife died."

"Okay. Well, two nights ago a nurse called Caroline and talked to her about Edna. I'm not sure exactly what the conversation was about, only that things weren't working out with Edna's care and there were problems. I guess her therapy wasn't progressing. That was about all Caroline said. Caroline insisted that the only way to solve the problem was for her to make another trip to Cold Springs." Mark took a drink of coffee measuring his words, reluctant to say too much to the Sheriff. "She had spent an entire month here and had just gotten back to Seattle a few weeks ago. The boys had missed her and complained about my cooking and were disappointed when she missed their ball games. But she insisted she had to come back here. She couldn't take care of it over the phone. Yes, we argued."

"When did Mrs. Archer leave for Cold Spring?" Jim took notes.

"She called that evening to make reservations. I think her plane left between nine or ten the next morning, yesterday. She flew Delta to Colorado Springs. That is what she usually does. Then rents a car. I think she had a layover in Denver." Mark started to tear up. "It was only yesterday. I called the boys last night. They were crying and screaming and I wasn't even there for them." Silence. "Janet, the neighbor lady had to comfort and calm them down. I need to be with them. I wasn't there for her either when she needed me." He wiped his eyes with his hand then pulled out his handkerchief for his nose.

"I know this is hard." The Sheriff put his pen down and sat back in his chair waiting for Mark to compose himself.

"Mr. Archer, what time did you leave Seattle?"

"I couldn't catch a plane out until one thirty. Had to fly to Denver then drive down here. I tried to call Caroline to tell her I was coming but she must have been in the air. Her cell phone went to voice mail."

"What time did you arrive in Denver?"

"Between four thirty and five. I took the toll road but still got caught in crosstown traffic." Mark took the ticket sub out of his pocket and laid it on the desk.

Hobson read the stub, made a couple of notes and handed it back. "Did you stop anywhere?"

"Yes, I stopped for gas and grabbed one of those pre-made sandwiches and coffee. I'm paranoid about getting stuck in the mountains and running out of gas. I always keep at least half a tank."

"Did you stop anywhere else?"

"No." Mark stuffed his handkerchief back in his pocket.

"Can you think of anywhere your wife would stop for dinner? You mentioned that she usually took Delta to Colorado Springs, then drove."

"Stopped?" After thinking a minute, "There's a place in Woodland Park, right off the highway. The boys always like to stop there because they make great milk shakes. She would have stopped there."

"You wouldn't remember the name of it would you?"

"I'm sorry, I don't."

"Do you have a picture of your wife?"

Opening his wallet, Mark shook his head in disappointment. "I'm sorry, just a picture of the boys." Taking the photo of his sons out, tears came to Mark's eyes again. Handing it to the Sheriff, he reached for a tissue from the box on the desk.

"Nice looking boys." The lawman commented, handing the photo back.

Looking over his notes, he mentioned, "I got the impression from what you said last night that Caroline didn't tell you exactly why she needed to come here?"

"No, she got a phone call from a nurse and when she hung up, she was upset. I'm not sure maybe she was only angry. Sometimes she's worried about something and is hard to read. She told me she had to go to Cold Springs to check on her mother and she wasn't sure how long she would be gone. I'm afraid that is when I got angry. She's been here so much and it was taking a toll on both the boys and me. I asked her why and she said that she needed to handle a couple of problems."

"She didn't give you any idea what the problems were?"

"No, when Caroline gets angry, she gets defensive and likes to be in control. Caroline takes her responsibility to her mother seriously and doesn't want my help. It's always been that way since we first got married."

Scattered thoughts were running through Mark's head, "I don't even know where she wants to be buried. We never talked about it. We both assumed that decision was a long way off. I guess I need to talk to Edna and the boys. If there is nothing else, I need to see Edna." Mark stood to leave but when he went to put the coffee cup on the desk, it slipped and hit the floor. It was empty, so nothing spilled.

"Sorry." He picked up his cup and set it on the desk.

The Sheriff thanked him for his help and left him assured he would be in touch. Mark walked out the office door and Jim wandered if he should allow him to drive. His coordination was not good; grief consumed his entire body.

After Mark left, Hobson called Warren. "Are you busy?"

His part-time deputy Warren answered

the phone. "No, not bad. Why? Do you need me to do something?"

"Yeah, would you go by Bristol's and see if she has a recent picture of her daughter? When you are there, find out what time she last talked to Caroline. Then go over to Woodland Park and ask around at the cafés. Find out if they saw Caroline anytime yesterday? She may have stopped at a place that makes great milkshakes. From what I can work out from a timeline, it took her a lot more than two hours to drive from the Colorado Springs airport to here. She should have gotten here by about four o'clock and she was shot about eight thirty. That is a lot of time missing. We need to find out what she was doing all that time."

"Great milkshakes in Woodland Park? Must be the Palace," he murmured. "I'll leave now. Talk to you later."

Sheriff Hobson's next called Mary Harris. "Mary, how is Mrs. Bristol, and are you still at her place?"

"I'm in my car driving home, Jim. I just left her place. Edna is doing okay. I gave her a sedative last night and slept on her couch. She slept fine. I fixed her breakfast, and we visited this morning. She's not taking Caroline's death well. I am aware it sounds strange but, Jim, I think she blames herself for Caroline getting killed. Makes no sense. I assured her it wasn't her fault, but she still insisted."

"Would she be up to me going out to talk to her today or should I wait 'til tomorrow?" The Sheriff wanted her professional opinion.

"I think she takes a nap about one. I would suggest about three o'clock?"

"What is your opinion of her housekeeper?"

"Now, Jim, you know how critical I can be about people, do you really want to hear what I think?"

"Yes, Mary, that is why I asked." Hobson smiled at his old friend.

"Well, Okay. I think Joyce is fat and lazy and puts her own comfort before everyone else's. I think she does the bare minimum taking care of Edna. I think the only reason she was given the job is because Edna and Caroline felt sorry for her. I visited with Joyce a little. Her daughter lives there too. She's from over by Gunnison and I found out we both worked with a nurse at Gunnison Memorial Hospital. Would you like me to talk to my friend there, about Joyce?"

"That would be a big help, Mary. Thanks." Mary confirmed for the Sheriff what Sarah had hinted at and what he had already concluded.

Hanging up the phone, Hobson stepped out of his office, "Dee, is Randy in yet?"

"He called, said he is on his way in. I got Kelly's robbery typed and entered into the system. I'm surprised he isn't robbed more often; being out in the middle of nowhere like that. Here is the bullet Randy took out of the shed." She gave him the plastic bag.

"Yeah, when Kelly calls us, it's usually a bar fight. However, he was robbed about three years ago, some biker thought he could hold up the place and get away. One of the regulars at Kelly's pulled in the lot when the guy took off on his bike. Arnold hollered from the door that they had been robbed. The guy followed the biker, and the biker sped up, missed the curve going downhill and flew off the road. The biker went to jail after he got out of the hospital and Kelly got his money back."

"Crime doesn't pay on crooked mountain roads." Dee turned back to her computer and her fingers flicked over the keyboard.

Clark arrived and he and Hobson went over the robbery details. "Do you think they suspect who did it?" The Sheriff's inquired.

"I think they have some guesses. But they wouldn't give me a name. I think the hesitancy is because the guy was small. Kelly and Arnold can't think of anyone with a slight build that knows enough about Kelly's habits to guess when he goes to the bank. And has enough guts to rob him."

The Sheriff sat in silence for a few minutes. "I can't believe I let Josh go out of state on vacation. Everything breaks loose when I'm short a deputy. I had to call in Warren to help with the murder. That is going to cost the taxpayers and the commissioners aren't going to be happy."

"Murphy's Law, Sheriff. Always happens. Kelly and Arnold should be in today to sign their statements. I'd like to sit in when you talk to them. I have a couple of questions."

\* \* \*

Warren pulled up in front of Edna's house on the outskirts of town. The tall grass choked the overgrown rose bushes beside the house. The rocks used to edge the rose bed hid in the bluegrass of what used to be the lawn. A lone snowball bush peaked through the lilacs on the border between the Bristol house and the one next door. The sidewalk remained in good shape. The foundation of a well-tended yard still existed.

He stepped on the porch, opened the screen and knocked on the heavy wooden door. Mark answered and invited Warren inside. Wiping his feet on the doormat before he entered, he was directed to the living room where Edna sat enjoying a cup of tea.

"Well, Warren, I didn't expect to see you today. How are you and your wife? How is Cary's father doing? I haven't seen Joe in ages."

"They're all just fine. How are you doing, Edna? I hate to intrude, but Sheriff Hobson asked me to stop by and see if you have a recent picture of Caroline." Warren stood holding his brown Stetson to his chest.

Pointing towards a framed photo of Caroline and her two sons on the old upright piano, "Will that one be okay? That's one of my favorites of her and the boys."

"Sure, that is a nice photo of Caroline. Can I take it out of the frame?" Warren picked up the photo, admired it then removed the heavy silver frame. "I promise I will take care of it and bring it back."

Joyce stood in the doorway. "I hate to interrupt, but I need to leave for a while. I need to take Tiffany to her car. That stupid girl ran out of gas on the Old Granger road last night and had to hitchhike home. I won't be long." She smiled, being on her best behavior in front of the stranger with the badge and Mark.

"That's fine, take your time. I will be here most of the afternoon." Mark watched his mother-in-law gave a hint of a smile. They would have peace and quiet while they visited. Funeral arrangements would be discussed, and they had several stories about Caroline to share. Edna had never been close to Mark; Caroline had always taken care of the things. Now her distance with Mark was being forced closed. They had to be there for each other, Caroline was gone.

"Thank you for the photo. If you need

anything, call me. I'll be leaving now. I'll show myself out." Warren nodded to Archer as he left.

* * *

Gathering information was the main part of any investigation and Jim Hobson called in favors for a positive start. The missing time between Colorado Springs and the shooting bothered him. Where had Caroline been? What had she been doing? He needed to know if anyone in Cold Springs had seen Caroline before the shooting. His first stop would be the local watering hole and information center on the town square.

Hobson remembered that two o'clock was after the noon rush and a slow time at the Wagon Wheel. Cliff Gordon was the owner and the most knowledgeable man in town as to current events, more commonly known as gossip. He had grown up here then joined the Air Force but had returned after his father's death in an auto accident. His inheritance turned out to be the bar and restaurant. The Sheriff always liked visiting the Wagon Wheel. It gave him a sense of continuity. It never changed, but then, few things in this small town did.

Walking in, he spied Cliff at his usual place behind the bar, dressed in his usual Levis and cotton western shirt with pearl snaps. He was about thirty, a little less than six feet and of medium weight, light brown hair, green eyes and a huge smile on his face.

The usual four elderly ranchers were at the back table playing poker with a half-empty pot of coffee sitting by the matchstick pile. Four straw, wide-brim Resistols hung from the old wooden pegs on the wall.

Cliff set a glass of iced tea in front of the Sheriff as he slid onto a barstool. "I heard about the shooting. Edna Bristol's daughter?"

"Yeah. Caroline Archer. Do you know her? Did you see her in here yesterday evening between four and eight thirty?"

"Yes, I would recognize her. But no. Well, I don't think I saw her in here. We had a good dinner rush last night. But, I don't think she was here. I've only seen her a few times when she was here with Edna over the years. She was a few years ahead of me in school, but I knew her to talk to her." Hobson could tell by the look on Cliff's face he was scanning his memory.

"Anything interesting on the wind? What was the topic of conversation at the ranchers morning coffee meeting?"

"The shooting is the main topic for everyone today. A lot of confusion in town as to who did it and why it happened. Most popular theory is that an outsider did it. Probably road rage or something."

A thought struck Cliff, "Oh, wait. You need to talk to Mrs. Demming out at the Stop N'

Go. She was in here at noon for takeout and mentioned she thought she had seen Caroline pull off into their parking lot."

"Okay, thanks, I'll talk to her. Have you met the woman that stays with Mrs. Bristol? Her name is Joyce Hunter?"

"No, I don't think I've met her. But I think it's her daughter that comes in here and keeps trying to convince me that she's twenty-one and can drink. Her name is Tiffany, and she's a real piece of work. She told me she lives with Edna. She comes in here on Friday and Saturday nights and sees who she can pick up. Tiffany seems to like guys with cowboy hats. I think I saw her leave one night with Chris England. If you want more information about her, you might check with Kelly. He would be more liable to fall for her line and serve her." The Wagon Wheel's competitor was Kelly's Lounge. They catered to a rougher crowd. "Tiffany is horse crazy too. You'd think she was only twelve years old the way she carries on about horses."

"Thanks, Cliff. And thanks for the tea. If you hear anything, call me." The Sheriff finished his tea and walked out the door in time to notice Kelly entering the courthouse.

Kelly had signed his statement when Hobson entered the reception area and motioned for Kelly and Randy to step into his office.

When the men were seated, Hobson asked, "Any idea who robbed you, Kelly?"

"I've told Clark everything I know." He gestured toward the deputy.

"Kelly, could this small person wearing a hoodie have been a woman?" Randy glanced at his boss.

"Are you suggesting one of my waitresses robbed me? No, Marsha is too tall. Cindy is way too heavy and Jessica . . . no, it wasn't her."

"How about a regular woman customer who knows your habits?" Hobson leaned back in his chair.

"A woman? I hadn't thought about that. The only words they said was 'giv' me' and 'shed'" He took a minute, "I don't know. I'll have to think about it."

The Sheriff read over Arnold's statement, "Can you think of a slight woman who drives a dark, small car and needs money?"

Kelly smiled, "Half of my women customers. Sorry, Sheriff, I wish I could help more."

\* \* \*

With a cup-to-go in hand, Hobson approached the cash register where Mrs. Demming was bent over a ledger, deep in thought. "You look busy."

"The oil company changed the way they bill us and it's driving me crazy. What can I help you with, Sheriff?" The petite, dark-haired thirty-year-old gave him a friendly smile.

The Stop N' Go was an old filling station that had been enlarged to accommodate a convenience store. Mrs. Demming's husband worked for the Rural Electric Association and they had two school age children. She helped her father run the store. On numerous occasions, she had tried to convince her father to sell the place, but that was his lifeline to the outside world and he planned on dying there. The town people would stop by for gas and a snack and visit with her dad. He had owned the station since before self-service. The checkout counter was in the front of the building, with a small section for automotive supplies. As you walked to the back, there were the soft drinks, chips, and various snack foods. The coffee and its additives were displayed in the back before you got to the restrooms. The huge windows in front of the store added to the overhead light making the cleanliness apparent.

"Cliff Gordon said you might have seen Caroline Archer, the lady who was killed last night?"

"Yeah, Edna's daughter. I don't know for sure it was her. I took out the trash about eight o'clock and saw a car pull off the road into the lot at the side of the building." The clerk motioned with her head to indicate the south side of the station. "I glimpsed a woman in a rental car, a Honda. She didn't buy gas or come inside. I assumed she was waiting for someone. She was just parked there. But from what I remember of Caroline, it looked like her."

"You didn't see anyone pull in beside her?"

"Sorry, Sheriff. No windows on that side of the building."

"Do you recall how long she parked there? When she pulled out?"

"I'm sorry, I didn't pay any attention," She shook her head clearly apologetic she couldn't be of further help.

"Would your dad have seen anything? How about someone else in the store?" He was desperate for clues about who Caroline might have been waiting for.

"Dad was home with a stomach virus." Sorting through her memory bank, she thought of something. "Warren Carpenter stopped by for gas, he came inside. I remember because he bought a candy bar and said he had missed dinner. I thought it was a long time after dinner and checked the clock. It was a little after eight." She smiled.

"Thanks, Mrs. Demming, I hope my deputy develops total recall."

\* \* \*

The waitress inside the restaurant in Woodland Park on Highway 24 gestured for Warren to take a seat as she filled a water glass and grabbed a menu.

Approaching the table and setting the glass and menu in front of Warren, "Can I get you something to drink?"

"I'll take a glass of iced tea and a piece of that strawberry-rhubarb pie." Warren had checked out the pie rack on his way in. He and his wife stopped for lunch here sometimes.

The waitress returned with his iced tea and pie. "Will there be anything else?"

"Yes." Warren showed her Caroline's photo. "Did you happen to notice this woman here yesterday evening?"

She studied the picture and frowned at Warren. He showed his badge.

"Look, I don't care what that stupid man said, that lady did nothing wrong!" The disgruntled waitress had her hands on her hips, daring him to dispute her words.

Warren held his hands up in surrender. "I'm not here about a complaint. Can you tell me what happened?"

The waitress sighed. "Sorry, but I am still angry about the whole thing. We were busy last night." Gesturing to the picture Warren had given her, she said, "I guess about six maybe six-thirty, this lady came in in a hurry. She whispered to me 'I'm double parked but I need to use the restroom.' Then ran back to the ladies room. A few minutes later this big heavy-set guy comes storming in demanding the driver of the

Honda 'move that damn car so I can pull out.'"
She mimicked his voice. "I went up to him and
nicely told him that I thought the driver was in
the ladies room and would be right out. That
didn't satisfy him. He wanted me to go into the
ladies room and 'drag her out'. I had my hand
full of dinner plates and was trying to wait on
customers. I didn't have time. Besides, I felt she
would be right out." She shook her head in
disgust. "This grown man, followed me across
the dining room throwing a fit and demanding
to see the manager. By this time, he had the
attention of all the diners and the other
waitresses. The manager wasn't here, so the
cook came out to handle the problem. The cook
had just approached the man when the woman
came out of the ladies room. When she realized
she had caused the problem. She apologized and
went right out and moved her car. The man
followed her outside. I asked the cook to keep an
eye on things. The cook followed them out to
their cars and waited for them both to drive
away." She frowned at Warren. "Well, if that
idiot didn't file some kind of complaint, why are
you here?"

Warren hated to tell her what had
happened to the lady. "Her name is Caroline
Archer. She was found shot last night in Cold
Springs."

"Oh, my goodness! You're kidding. That
nice lady? No. No," she shook her head. Then

suddenly stopped, "Do you think that crazy guy did it?" Her eyes got big.

"I don't know what to think. Do you think he could have been angry enough to follow her and shoot her?" Warren wanted her opinion.

The waitress turned around, mumbled "just a minute," and ran off.

She hollered at someone and came back a few minutes later with a man in tow. Judging by the apron, Warren guessed he was the cook from last night.

"You tell this deputy about what happened to that lady last night," she ordered.

The cook was what everyone imagined a short-order cook at a diner would look like. He was in his forties, big, bald with a small mustache and wrapped in a stained white apron. He held out his beefy paw of a hand to Warren and they shook. Warren explained about Caroline and this surprised the cook.

"Do I think Alan could have hurt that woman? No. I know the guy. He was upset last night. He makes a lot of noise but he wouldn't hurt anyone especially not a woman. I followed them out to the parking lot. She moved her car; he got in his pickup and left. She was still in her car as he headed up the hill. He's short tempered since he was laid off from his mechanics job last month. If you want to talk to him, he lives on up the mountain about ten miles."

Warren had his notepad out. "What's his name?"

"Alan Bennett. He lives off 24 on 67, small house painted white with blue trim. He didn't do it." The adamant cook shook his head as he walked back to the kitchen. Warren thanked the waitress, paid for his order and left.

Sitting in his truck, he called Hobson. After explaining last night's confrontation, he asked if the Sheriff wanted him to talk to Alan Bennett. Warren could almost hear him mulling over the facts he had given him. Warren reiterated, "The cook was certain this guy had a short temper but cooled down fast, and he would never hurt a woman. He was pretty convincing." Finally, the Sheriff decided not to question the man yet and Warren went back to Cold Springs.

* * *

Deputy Clark was waiting for Hobson when he returned to his office. Following the Sheriff into his private office, "The rental car is at Shorty's garage. Caroline rented the car at 4:43 yesterday at the Colorado Springs airport. I found her cell phone under the seat. She had three missed calls from her husband at various times of the day. It doesn't look like any of them were returned. It looks like she made one call to Edna before she got on the plane. At 5:08 she received a call from Bristol's phone, it lasted less than two minutes. Another call from Bristol's again at 7:20 – it lasted over four minutes. There was another call after that but I couldn't track the number. It was probably from a disposable phone." Randy sat in the chair across from the Sheriff with his papers laid out.

"She only made the one call after she left Seattle?"

"Just the one to Edna early in the morning. After that, nothing. Not on her cell anyway. Oh, the passenger side mirror is cracked on that rental car. It looks like there is white paint on it."

"Minor accident?" Hobson leaned back in his chair.

"Don't know. I'll call the rental place but I don't think they'd rent a car with a broken mirror."

"I agree. Warren is finished in Woodland Park. He's going back to his ranch. He'll be in first thing tomorrow. Let's start a timeline going and see what we have." The Sheriff checked his call notes. Clark brought in the whiteboard from the break-room and cleaned it off.

Murder investigations were something the Sheriff of this sparsely populated county didn't encounter often. This was only the fourth one of his career in Cimarron County. In two of them, the murderer had been standing over the victim as witnesses arrived. The other one was an accident and was solved within a few days by a remorseful uncle's confession. This would be different; Hobson felt it in his bones.

# CHAPTER 5

"Good Morning, Sheriff's Office. Randy Clark speaking." Sitting with his feet on his desk, he gazed out the window at the bright new day.

A panicked woman's voice hollered out of the phone. "Randy, this is Debbie Ehman. Angie is missing. I guess she ran away from home. She took her horse."

He pulled his feet off the desk and sat up straight in his chair. Fumbling through the mass of papers he had been getting ready to restack, he found a pen and his yellow legal tablet. He remembered Debbie and thought he would recognize her daughter too.

"Okay. Debbie, calm down. How long has she been gone?"

"I'm not sure, I guess since sometime last night. When I went to wake her up this morning, her bed hadn't been slept in."

"I assume she owns a cell phone, and you called it?"

After a brief silence and a long sigh, "She doesn't have her cell with her. She threw a fit, slammed the door to her bedroom so hard it cracked the frame; I got angry and took her phone away. It's in my nightstand."

"Okay. You called all her friends, right? She'sn't hanging out with a girl friend?"

"No, no. I've called all her friends and even her teacher. No one has seen her since yesterday evening. I even called my ex to see if he had heard from her. No one has heard from her." She sobbed into a handful of tissue muffling her voice.

"Okay, I need some information. How old is Angie?"

"She'll be twelve in October."

"You say she took her horse? What kind?" the deputy shook his head.

"An eight-year-old buckskin gelding. We bought it from Ross Campbell."

An image of the retired cutting horse filled his mind. "Ross's gelding that had hock problems?"

"Yeah, that one."

"Look, Debbie, you need to come into town and file a report and bring a photo of both her and the horse. Okay?"

"I'm on my way!" Debbie said and hung up.

Randy put the phone down as Hobson walked in the office. "Good morning, Sheriff. We have an eleven-year-old runaway on a buckskin gelding."

Without breaking his stride, the Sheriff responded, "Good mornin', Randy. No, I have a murder investigation. You have an eleven-year-old runaway." He flung his Stetson on the hat rack by the door and proceeded to the break room and found Dee making coffee. "Who is it?" he called back over his shoulder.

"Angie Ehman, Debbie's daughter. Debbie will be in shortly with a photo and I hope more information." The deputy hollered back.

"How long has she been gone?" Hobson turned and walked back into the waiting area with his coffee.

"Since sometime last night."

He shook his head and continued into his office, "Tell me when Debbie gets here."

"Yes, sir." Randy met Warren coming out of the break room. They both went into the sheriff's private office. The beginning of Caroline Archer's timeline was written on the whiteboard.

Friday Night:

Caroline received call from Mary about Edna

Caroline called Edna to tell her she was coming.

Saturday:

10:30 Caroline called again and spoke to her mother.

10:50 Left Seattle

2:20 Arrived Denver

3:10 Left Denver

4:20 Arrived Colorado Springs

4:43 Rented Car

5:08 Received phone call from the Bristol

house
6/6:30 Woodland Park confrontation
7:20 Received a 4 min call from Bristol's phone again (Should have been in Cold Springs.)
8:10 Call from disposable phone
8:20 Stopped at Stop N' Go – White pickup
8:36 Shooting

Warren took the remaining chair across from the Sheriff and nodded to Randy, now in the adjacent chair. All three stared at the board. "The only thing I see is -- if she left Woodland Park at six-thirty, she should have been in Cold Springs by seven-thirty? There was no weather problem, it wouldn't have taken her more than an hour. She must have been here for at least an hour before she was shot?"

Randy ventured an opinion. "For immediately jumping on a plane, she didn't break any speed limits getting here."

Warren stared at the board. "Maybe every time she got a call she pulled off the road to talk?" His wife would do that if she knew the conversation would be long or complicated.

"What are your thoughts on the confrontation in Woodland Park, Warren?" Hobson eyed his part-time deputy.

"I think the guy was agitated at having his car blocked and not being able to leave. I don't think it was any more than that. Road rage doesn't last an hour and a half. The cook knew the guy, and he doesn't seem to think he would do anything like that."

"It doesn't look like she was in a real hurry to get here. It's only a two-hour drive from Colorado Springs. And she chose a plane with a layover. It could have been the only flight available." Hobson mumbled.

"Have you talked to Edna about the phone calls?" Clark turned toward the Sheriff.

"No, I've been giving her time to accept her daughter's death. I will go out this afternoon. Randy, why don't you go with me? You can visit with Joyce Hunter, the woman who takes care of Edna."

He gave a nod and Hobson asked, "Warren, I talked to Mrs. Demming at the Stop N' Go. She said you stopped in there about the time she thinks she saw Caroline's car in the parking lot. Do you remember seeing her car parked over at the side of the building?"

"Well, let me think. Yes, I pulled into the parking lot from the side street and remember a car parked by the building. It sure could have been Caroline's Honda. There was a light colored pickup truck that pulled in behind me. I went on around to the front of the building and went inside."

He paused, "I don't remember the truck following me around to the front. I'm sure it didn't. I was the only customer inside. The pickup wasn't there when I came out. The parking lot was empty except for my truck. I didn't look around the side of the building when I left, I pulled directly onto the highway."

The Sheriff wanted more information. "What do you remember about the white pickup?"

"Its headlights were on as it pulled in behind me. I only noticed it was white when I turned the corner of the building. It was a late model pickup, Dodge . . . maybe a Toyota. Sorry, anything else would only be a guess." Warren frowned and scratched his head.

"Didn't hear any loud noise like the pickup bumping Caroline's car?" Randy thought about the white paint on the mirror.

"No." Warren shook his head.

The phone rang and Dee picked up. "Sheriff's office, Dee speaking."

She listened for a second and motioned for someone to pick up the extension. "One moment, please. Let me have you speak to a deputy."

"Randy Clark."

"Hi, this is Dave Watson. I got an extra horse in my pasture. A sorrel mare that doesn't belong to me."

"Hi, Dave. You mean you found a buckskin gelding." His mind flashed back to the runaway and her horse.

"No, Randy!" He gave a long huff. "I know a sorrel mare from a buckskin gelding!

I've got someone's sorrel mare in my pasture, eatin' my newly cut hay! What in the hell are you talking about a buckskin for?"

"Sorry, Dave. We have an eleven-year-old runaway on a buckskin gelding were looking for. You say you have an extra mare in your pasture?"

"Yes, this is not my horse. I found her in my front pasture this morning. I checked for any downed fences but couldn't find any. The only way for her to get in would have been for someone to open my gate and put her there. The gate has a combination lock on it but my family doesn't remember to lock it half the time. She's eating my newly cut hay. I took a picture of her with my cell phone. What's your email address, I'll send it to you."

The deputy rattled off the address, went out to his desk and hit a button on the computer to check his email. The computer dinged.

"Got it. Does she have a number?"

"No. No brand or lip tattoo either. When you find the owner, tell him I'm charging him to board his damn horse."

"Dave, no one called in a missing horse. I'll call the vet offices, email the photo and see if they recognize her." He hung up and turned to the dispatcher, "I've never been told that one before."

"What one?" he had Dee's attention, and she turned away from her computer, a frown mark between her striking blue eyes.

"Dave Watson has an extra sorrel mare in his pasture."

"And he's complaining? He needs some new blood in that string of his."

"Maybe so, but she's dining on his freshly cut hay."

Dee turned back to her computer, slowly shaking her long dark ponytail. "Oh, naughty, naughty girl!"

Warren gave the others a wave on his way out of the office.

\* \* \*

The Sheriff got a call back from his friend Jeff Sherman in Seattle. "Mark Archer is an engineer and works for TechCon Consulting. They contract with several high-tech companies in this area. He and his wife live in an upper middle-class neighborhood and have two boys. Archer is in good standing with his company and they are anxious for him to return to work. He left on emergency leave in the middle of a contract. They aren't aware of any home problems except for Caroline's mother's illness. I talked to three of the neighbors; two of them thought their marriage was on solid ground. The other neighbor woman is a close friend of Caroline's. She said Caroline had complained about Mark working so much and how she hated living in Seattle. Caroline wanted to move back to Denver so she could be closer to her mother. Caroline hadn't mentioned divorce to the neighbor, but she was very unhappy. She worked contract labor, and she wasn't always employed, this also put stress on the marriage. As far as the neighbor knows they do not cheat on each other and their boys are exceptional kids most of the time. One other thing, the neighbor mentioned that Caroline was usually very laid back, but she didn't handle stress well. When she was stressed, little things got blown way out of proportion. At least that was her friend's opinion."

"Okay, thanks. I'll return the favor anytime I can."

"Also, in the last seven years she's paid two parking tickets, and he had a speeding ticket in a school zone. They are up to date on their property taxes. Anything else you want to know?"

"No, I think you have covered everything. I appreciate your help. If I can help you anytime, call me." The Sheriff hung up and wrote a couple of notes in the file. He had a few more questions to ask Mark but they could wait until he talked to Edna.

The Sheriff caught excited voices coming from the reception area and went to listen.

Randy sat behind his desk and Debbie Hudson and her older sister were seated in the chairs in front. They were in the open area behind the reception desk.

"Okay Debbie, tell me what happened last night."

Debbie turned seeking her sister for support. The tall woman, Gail nodded her head. "Angie and I got into an argument. Her dad came to pick her up for her weekend with him. We're divorced. Have been for two years, he has her two weekends a month. This is his weekend to have her. He came out to the house, and he had been drinking. He wasn't drunk, but he is not to drink at all when he has her. I wouldn't let her go with him. He was angry when he left, but he did leave. She was angry because I wouldn't let her go. She didn't understand that he had been drinking and shouldn't be driving. We got into a fight, an argument, and I sent her to her room."

"I didn't know she was missing until this morning when I went to wake her up. Her bed wasn't slept in." Debbie finished.

"You and Angie live with your sister don't you?"

Both sisters nodded their heads. "Yes, we live with Gail and her husband, Trevor."

"Did you talked with your ex-husband this morning? Has he seen her?"

"Yes, I called him first thing this morning. He hasn't seen her. He lives in Canon City and drives a long haul truck. The dispatcher called him at five this morning to take a load to Salt Lake City. Since he wouldn't have Angie for the weekend, he took it. He was already on the road when I called."

"Can you give me his phone number and address? You said she took her horse?" He entered the information into his computer.

Debbie handed him a slip of paper with the information.

"Yes. A buckskin gelding. I think her sleeping bag and coat are also gone."

"You said you called all of her friends? No one has heard from her?"

"No." Debbie's voice trembled, and she wiped tears from her eyes.

Hobson leaned against his doorway, "Does she go camping with anyone?"

"Yes, her dad took her and Vanessa Campbell to the National Forest one time but Van's dad took them several times. Do you think that is where she's?" Hope filled Debbie's face.

"Let's call Mr. Campbell, find out where he camps and check it out." Randy picked up the phone. "You are talking about Ross Campbell?"

"Yes. His number is on here." Debbie handed him another sheet of paper with a list of names and numbers of Angie's friends. She had called all of them this morning early, getting several out of bed.

Randy knew Ross. He had a few cattle but made most of his money as a fall hunting guide in the National Forest.

Debbie, her sister, and the Sheriff listened to the Deputy's side of the conversation but waited for a thorough explanation when he finished.

Putting the receiver down, Clark told them. "Well, Ross took them to three different camp sites. He doesn't think she could find two of them on her own but he is on his way to check all three. He had already left the house when Debbie called. He just found out that Angie was missing as I called. He said he would stop by the ranger station on his way in to tell them what was happening. Now, did you bring a photo of Angie and the buckskin? I can fax it to the ranger station along with the sheriff's offices in the neighboring counties."

"Make extra copies and give them to Dee to hand out to the ranchers who have their morning coffee at the Wagon Wheel. Tell them they need to be on the lookout for a young girl on a buckskin," Hobson suggested.

"Okay, a horse walking will do about four miles per hour. Assuming the girl hasn't just walked the horse all time, she's probably within twenty miles of her house." Randy looked at the people around him for confirmation.

The others shook their heads in agreement. Gail, Angie's aunt, verbalized what the others were thinking. "I don't think she would go any further than that. She's not familiar with this area. She's familiar with maybe eight miles around our place and then the places in the National Forest. Angie knows how to get into town. I can't imagine her taking off in a unfamiliar direction."

"I'll call Warren and Darrell and send them out to Debbie's place on horses and see if they can track Angie. Randy, when you're finished contacting the Ranger station, I want you to go to the Forest and check the picnic and camping areas near the entrance." The Sheriff went into his office to call his part-time deputies.

* * *

Mary Harris got the casserole dish out of her car and detected loud voices coming from Edna's house. The wooden front door was open and Mary opened the screen door and peeked into the foyer. The voices were coming from the living room.

"I can't loan you any more money, Joyce. I don't have it," Edna's muffled voice cried.

"I don't need much; five hundred will do. I just can't make my insurance payment on my car. That means I can't drive to the store for food or your pain pills." Joyce's loud angry voice answered Edna's plea.

"Why can't Tiffany pick up my medication? She lives here, too."

"I don't get paid for running your

errands!" Tiffany exclaimed.

"I thought Caroline was paying you a monthly salary plus covering all the food and car expenses."

"No, it doesn't cover everything! And now Caroline is dead. Who do you think is going to take care of you? Huh? Do you think that worthless son of your gives a damn about you? Is he going to come home from the army to take care of you?"

Mary could make out Edna sobbing while Joyce berated the situation. "It's going to be me taking care of you so you had better start getting along with me. And quit your damn crying. I hate that."

Mary had listened to all she could take. She closed the screen door and knocked loud enough to halt the conversation inside.

Joyce came to the door in baggy slacks and an old t-shirt. "What do you want?"

"I came to visit Mrs. Bristol." Mary pushed her way through the doorway and went to the living room. Edna sat in a chair with her walker in front of her, eyes red with a tissue to her face.

"Hi, how are you doing?" Mary sat on the edge of the chair beside Edna.

Looking nervously at Joyce, She gave a half smile, "I'm fine."

"Look, Edna. I brought my ham casserole. The one you like so much." Mary showed her the dish.

She glanced at Joyce. "We don't eat ham. Tiffany doesn't like it."

Joyce folded her arms over her ample chest and left the room.

"I didn't bring this for Tiffany, Edna, I brought it for you," Mary gritted her teeth. Then turning to look at Tiffany she saw a blue cashmere sweater stretched around her shoulders as she left the room.

"Edna, is that the sweater you wore to the Christmas party? The one Caroline gave you for your birthday?" Mary remembered how nice she looked in that shade of blue.

"Joyce told me it looked better on Tiffany. So I gave it to her," Edna's head went down as her eyes followed the young girl out of the room.

"Are you hungry? Would you like some of the casserole now?"

Without answering, Edna struggled to stand. Mary set down the dish and helped her onto her walker so she could start down the hall to her room. She motioned towards the casserole. Mary picked it up and followed the slow moving walker. In the bedroom, she motioned for Mary to close the door as she reached into the nightstand and pulled out a fork and small saucer.

"Barbara down the street brought me blueberry cobbler yesterday."

Mary smiled as she saw the utensil and

helped Edna sit on the bed so she could use the nightstand as a table. Edna gave her a big smile and placed a spoonful of casserole on the plate. Mary pulled the chair up beside the bed and smiled.

"You were still sleeping when I left. Did the muscle relaxant I gave you help you sleep?"

Swallowing her second bite, "Yes, I did just fine. I can't believe Caroline is dead. When she called, she mentioned she wanted to come home. But she didn't say when she was coming. She was only here a few weeks ago. I don't understand why she was coming back so soon."

"I spoke to her." Mary worried how her friend would receive the news.

"What? Why?" Edna's face didn't register concern as much as fear.

"Sarah Howard is concerned that you weren't exercising your leg, and you weren't eating well." Mary put it as nicely as she could. She actually just wanted to tell her what she thought of Joyce.

Shaking her head with, "Oh, Mary, you shouldn't have done that. Joyce will be angry." The implication in her voice was that Joyce's anger would be taken out on her.

"I'm sorry, I've upset you. I didn't mean to do that." Mary sighed.

Edna nodded and timidly took another bite.

After a few minutes of watching her eat,

Mary smiled, "Are you enjoying the casserole?"

"Yes, you are one of the best cooks in town, Mary. How are things going at the hospital? Did they repair the wall?"

"Yes, I still can't believe that man drove his car right into the side of the building trying to get his wife to the hospital in time. They were just lucky they all weren't hurt. It didn't do much damage to the wall but his car was sure a mess. But they have twin boys now. I hope the father isn't the one to teach them to drive." Mary laughed and Edna smiled as she finished eating.

"Edna, I didn't see old Bugler as I came in. Do you still have him?"

"I don't know." Edna was worried. "I haven't seen that old basset hound in several days. Would you take a look and see if you can find him? I would feel terrible if anything happened to him. Caroline and Robert both loved that dog. When Robert died, Bugler howled for three days. I thought the neighbors would complain to the Sheriff, but they understood that he just missed Robert."

"Your husband thought a lot of that dog. I'll look for him when I leave. I'm sure he is around here somewhere."

"Joyce doesn't like dogs. She won't let him in the house anymore." Edna wiped off her fork with a tissue and put it back in the nightstand.

"I need to go now. I need to be at the

hospital in half an hour. I'll put the rest of the casserole in your refrigerator and you can eat more later." Mary gave her friend a hug, picked up the food pan and took it to the kitchen. The room was empty, so she put it in the refrigerator and went out the back door.

Mary searched the yard and called to the dog for several minutes before a neighbor came out of the back of his house and walked toward her. Meeting him at the back chain link fence, "Have you seen a Basset hound?"

"Do you mean old Bugler?"

"Yes, Mrs. Bristol's dog."

"I've been meaning to go over and tell Edna, I buried him two days ago. I found him in the bushes over there." He pointed to the corner of his property. "He dug his way under the fence like he always does. Only this time I think he was poisoned. The dog was dead when I found him. I mentioned this to the woman who lives there with her and she informed me that 'no one cared about the damn dog'."

Mary closed her eyes and shook her head. "Thank you for taking care of the dog. I'll let Edna know. You think he was poisoned?"

"There was still foam around his mouth when I found him and his body was contorted. I saw that sort of thing once before when I was out on a ranch and a dog got hold of rat poison. I probably should have taken him to the vet before I buried him."

"That's okay. You did the right thing. I have a feeling he was poisoned." Mary walked back to the house and entered by the back door.

She picked up her purse and went through the living room as Joyce commented, "I thought you already left."

"No, I'm just leaving." Mary held her tongue and walked to her car. She started the car and headed directly for the Western Star Motel where Mark stayed.

## CHAPTER 6

Randy traveled slowly along Highway 832, looking first out one side window then the other. He phoned Warren and Darrell, the part-time deputies, who were now on their way to Debbie's ranch. He told them he was going to talk with the forest ranger. After an hour, he had only passed one other truck, a local rancher who did the four-fingers steering wheel wave. He pulled onto the blacktop picnic area parking near the Forest entrance and got out of his pickup to check for hoof prints.

Along the perimeter in back he found two u-shaped dimples in the wet leaves. They were horse prints but he couldn't tell how old they were.

The deputy had been examining the ground for several minutes when movement behind the furthest table caught his eye. He walked towards a tan shape behind some pines. He thought it might be the buckskin.

He called out. "Angie? Angie!"

Randy caught a rustling noise, and a shot rang out.

He dove for protection under the concrete table, and hit his knee, sending a jolt of pain up his leg. His head spun from the pain and the thought that someone shot at him. He was sure the noise was a gunshot.

A whinny confirmed the tan mass was a horse. The deputy lifted his head in time to see it disappear. Someone hollered and chased after it.

He assumed he had found the runaway, but she was fleeing.

Randy stood and hollered, "Angie, come here! I just want to talk! Angie! Angie!"

The pair crashed through the trees, the noise moving away from him.

The deputy hurriedly limped in the direction of the commotion, listening to the retreating hoof beats. He knew he couldn't catch her on foot.

"Dammit."

He was not sure which bothered him more, the pain in his leg or letting Angie escape. He was still confused about the gunshot.

He rubbed his knee and hobbled back to his pickup. As he opened the passenger side door to reach for his radio, he found a deep dent in the metal roof. He radioed to Dee and told her to put Hobson on the line. He quickly explained that he had found the girl, but she shot at him and got away.

"Jeez . . shit," Hobson mumbled. "Deputy, are you telling me we have an eleven-year-old run away with a gun shooting at my deputies?"

"Yes, sir. That is exactly what I am telling you." Disgusted, Randy studied the crease the bullet had put in the roof of his new Dodge Ram.

"Tell me exactly what happened."
Hobson reached for his hat thinking he would
go help, then changed his mind and sat back
down.

"Before I went into the National Forest to
meet the ranger, I stopped at the rest area beside
the creek just before the entrance. When I got out
of my pickup, I checked for hoof prints then I
caught movement behind some trees. It looked
like the buckskin the kid had taken off on. I tried
getting close, I hollered and called her name. The
next thing I knew, I was dodging a bullet. The
gunshot scared the horse, and he took off. The
kid ran after it. I chase her. When the sound of
hooves was gone, I came back to my truck and
phoned you."

"Shit. I'll send Warren and Darrell out to
help you find her. I'll tell the ranger what is
going on and that the kid has a GUN. I'm going
out to talk to her mother. Where in the hell did
an eleven-year-old get a gun?"

"Sheriff, have Warren and Darrell bring
their horses and an extra one for me. We are
going to need them. What are your thoughts
about calling in the Cimarron County Rescue or
the Highway Patrol?"

"I'll call Capt. Lambert with HP and him
bring him up to date on what's happening. I hate
to use Rescue for this; someone might get hurt."

Randy hung up with the Sheriff and got
in his pickup as a giant black F250 pulled in

beside him.

"What in the hell are you shooting at?" Ross Campbell leaned out his truck window glaring at Randy.

The deputy hollered back, "I'm not shooting at anyone! That kid, Angie Ehman, just took a shot at me!"

"What?" Ross got out of his truck and went over to talk to Clark. "Now what is going on?"

He explained events to Ross. "She just left here? Which way did she go?" Ross studied the area for any sign of Angie or her gelding through the thick trees edging the forest. Paths led away from the picnic area but most of them didn't go far. The real hiking and riding trails were deeper onto the Federal land.

The deputy pointed to the west, beyond the picnic table. "The horse took off that way but from what I could tell by his hoof beats, I think he turned north. The girl was running after him."

Ross was mapping this out in his head, "Okay, there is a small clearing a quarter of a mile north of here. I'll take the Forest road and check that one while you wait for the other deputies and the horses. I've got my cell. I will keep in touch. She has a gun? I assume a handgun. Right? That kid is not big enough for much of a gun. Could it have been a .22 rifle?"

"I don't think so. This is the crease it

made in my cab." The deputy ran his finger over the dent.

Both men quickly examined the dent and agreed it had to come from a large caliber handgun. "I'll check the clearing; if I don't find her, maybe I will find tracks. I'll let you know. I've already been by one of the campsites the girls and I use to go to. I didn't find any sign of her." Ross got into his pickup and headed up into the forest.

Randy pulled up his pant leg and checked his knee where an extensive bruise started to color. He got on the radio and was assured by Warren that he and Darrell were on his way with two horses. Warren told him the Sheriff had contacted the Ranger and he would meet them at his house. They could use one of his horses. The deputy relayed where Ross Campbell would check and he would be waiting for them at the picnic area where he had last seen Angie.

***

The part-time deputies pulled into the picnic area with a horse trailer attached and saw Clark on his cell phone. Warren and Darrell had ridden the rodeo circuit together then gone into semi-retirement about the same time. Warren had gone back to Cimarron County where he was born and raised. A few months later Darrell, the Texan, bought a ranch outside of Cold Springs, too. Now they were ranchers and on-call deputies when they were needed. Warren was a few inches taller than Darrell but they both had the same sturdy build.

Randy received a call from Ross at the clearing. Angie was not there, but he found hoof tracks leading down a trail deeper into the Forest. They quickly decided their next stop would be the Ranger's to pick up two more horses. They would meet Ross at the clearing. It was lucky that Darrell had insisted on taking his extended-cab truck with the four-horse trailer instead of Warren's smaller one.

The Ranger Station was seven miles onto government land and the rangers' house and corral were another hundred yards off the paved road. When they pulled up to the corral, a sorrel gelding was saddled and waiting for them. The ranger walked out of his house and joined them.

"Any idea where the girl is? Does she really have a gun?" the ranger opened the corral gate.

"Yeah, she really has a gun!" Randy pulled out a forest map spread it on the pickup hood and indicated the area. "Ross Campbell found hoof prints at the clearing over here."

Remembering the area, the Ranger said, "That's a big clearing with four trails leading off from it. Did he say which one she took?"

"No, we are to meet him there with an extra horse," Clark explained.

The Ranger glanced at the three men,

"Okay, I see three men plus Ross, I guess you'll need two more horses."

With a nod from Randy, Warren and Darrell went to the tack room for gear. The ranger took a halter off the gate, entered the corral and put the halter on a little bay mare. Leading her out, he stopped and held her while Warren and Darrell saddled her up. Randy led the already saddled sorrel, out of the corral and loaded him in with the bay and Warren's two horses.

"I'll be in the office for another three hours, then another ranger will relieve me and I can come help if you need me. Keep in touch so we will know where you are. Watch out for hikers and campers, several cars came in this morning before you called. I'll stop anyone else from going in until you find her. Tell us when you catch the little brat." The ranger went to set up the bright orange cones to block the road.

"Will do!" Randy shouted as he slid into the passenger side of Darrell's truck as it drove to the clearing.

***

Dee was always alert to the happenings in her domain; she felt it was part of her job description as dispatch/office assistant. When the Sheriff came out of his back office for another cup of coffee, "Did I hear the Hudson girl shot at

Randy? Is he okay?"

"Yeah, he's fine. Let me get my coffee and cool off, then I need to call Debbie Ehman." He glanced out the window at the bright sunshine. "Thank God it's not hunting season," he growled and disappeared into the break-room.

Two minutes later, he stood in the reception area grumbling to himself. "Yes, it seems that our eleven-year-old run away has a gun and used it to shoot at Randy!"

He stomped back into his office.

"I'm going on lunch break," Dee cried out, grabbing her purse and going out the door. She didn't want to be in hearing distance when the Sheriff reached Angie's mother.

Hobson took deep breaths as he waited for Debbie to answer the phone.

"Hello."

"Debbie Ehman?"

"Yes," Debbie said cautiously. She could hear the man on the line was holding back a lot of anger.

"Mrs. Ehman, this is Sheriff Hobson. You forgot to tell me that your daughter got hold of a gun. I take it one is missing from your home?"

"What? My daughter has a gun?"

"Yes, and your daughter just took a shot at one of my deputies. Would you like to explain where she got the gun?"

"My daughter doesn't have a gun! Except for Trevor's hunting rifles, there are no guns in this house. Those rifles are kept under his bed in a locked gun safe. Wait. Hold on." He heard her put the phone down.

Minutes later, a panting Debbie came back on the line, "The gun safe and guns are still locked under the bed. Are you sure she has a gun? She doesn't know how to use a gun."

"Yes, Debbie, she has a gun. We're sure it is Angie. Randy Clark was at the picnic area just outside the forest when he recognized the horse, hollered at Angie and she shot at him."

Trying to understand and kick her mind in gear to absorb what was happening, "Oh, my god! Sheriff, I have no idea where she got the gun. She doesn't know about shooting. She's never been around guns. You said she's up by the National Forest? Gail, Trevor and I want to help, we'll meet you there. We can help look for her."

"No, we can handle this. The deputies think they know where to find her and we have horses and a tracker up there. Besides, Ross Campbell is with them."

"Yes, his wife called and told me he took off for the camping areas to look for her as soon as he heard she was missing. Are you sure we can't come help, Sheriff? This waiting is driving me crazy."

"I'm sorry, Debbie, but since she has a gun, I only want my deputies looking for her. I have the highway patrol on standby. If we don't find her by nightfall, they will send troopers to help search. Meanwhile, would you call your friends and find out if anyone knows how she got a gun and what kind and how much ammunition she might have." Hobson's headache worsened.

"Oh, my god! Sheriff, would someone shoot my daughter? No! No!" The reality of her daughter's danger shook Debbie's world.

"Debbie!" He shouted into the phone, "My deputies would never fire a weapon at a child! You can depend on that!" Then in a soothing voice, "But, that is also why I can't allow anyone except law enforcement officers help with this search. Do you understand?"

Between sobs, she said, "Yes. Yes, I do."

"Okay, does your husband own any guns? Could she have taken one from him?"

"He keeps a handgun in his running bag because he drives by himself. But, he keeps extra money in it too, so he has a combination lock on it. I don't think she even knows about it. I'll call him and ask."

"Call anyone you can think of who owns a gun. Find out how she could have gotten hold of it. I'll tell you immediately anything we find out about Angie. You do the same, Debbie." His authoritarian voice got the cooperation he wanted.

"I will, Sheriff. I will." Debbie hung up and called her husband's cell. He didn't answer, so she left a panicked voice mail.

* * *

The Western Star Motel had twelve units. Built in the 1960's of brick with white wood trim, it still looked nice and inviting. Mary stopped at the office to inquire what room Mark had booked before going down the walk to unit Eight.

Mark opened the door after her knock. "Well, hi. Mary, right?" he was not sure about the etiquette of inviting a woman into his motel room in a small town.

"Yes, Mary Harris. Mark, could we go to the Wagon Wheel and have coffee and talk?"

"Of course, let me grab my jacket." He disappeared into the room worried there was another problem he would be forced to deal with and in his state of mind, he was not sure he could. Putting on his jacket, he pulled the door shut and tried to smile.

The real conversation didn't start until they were seated in a booth at the Wagon Wheel and were waiting for their drinks.

Mary spits out the sentence she had been rehearsing on the way over. "You are aware of how sorry I am about Caroline and I don't want to add to your problems, but I was out checking on Edna and overheard Joyce asking her for money."

Mark frowned, "I don't understand. I

thought Caroline paid her in advance the first of every month. I'm sure she told me it included an amount for food and gas."

The waitress serving their drinks interrupted them. They waited for her to leave.

"You might want to check with Edna." Mary hated having this conversation with Mark. She felt a husband should be able to mourn the death of his wife without having to deal with more problems. "Maybe you should stay at Edna's house."

"Yes, I probably should. I visited this morning for an hour or so and we talked about funeral services. When they release Caroline's body." His voice shook, and he reached for his drink. "I don't think there's an extra room. Joyce and her daughter use two of the bedrooms and the other is used for storage. Besides, what little time I spent out there today put my nerves on end. Joyce would not turn off the TV set and the daughter had music blaring. Edna and I could barely talk."

"I need to tell you one other thing then. I may have a solution but I need to talk to Doctor Levine first." Mary took a few sips of coffee she felt like she was tattling. "Do you remember Edna's dog? His name was Bugler?"

Mark nodded his head, and she continued. "I talked to her neighbor, he found the dog poisoned and buried him. I haven't told Edna yet. She thinks he just ran off. Edna mentioned Joyce didn't like the dog."

"Do you think Joyce poisoned the dog?" He couldn't believe anyone would do such a thing.

Mary stared down at her coffee. "I don't know. But, it did cross my mind."

"I guess I could go out and fire Joyce but then who would look after Edna? I can't think about any of this right now. I'm sorry. My mind is a muddle. I should be doing things but I just can't think about anything but Caroline." His voice broke, and he reached in his back pocket for a handkerchief.

They sat in silence. Finally, Mark spoke, "You said you might have a solution to some of these problems? What did you mean?"

"I need to talk to Doctor Levine first. But since she'sn't making any progress with walking, he might agree to put her back in the rehab part of the hospital for a week or two. It would get her away from Joyce and help her and put her on a better rehab schedule. She's way behind on her rehab. The longer things draw out the harder it gets."

"Do you think he would agree to that? Edna has a good Medicare supplement to take care of the cost. Caroline showed me the bill when she got out of rehab and I was surprised at how little it was."

"I'll call Doctor Levine right now." Mary left the booth and stepped outside.

When she returned minutes later, she had a big smile, "Doctor Levine is thinking along the same lines, but strictly because Edna wasn't making progress at home. He checked and they have two empty beds. He will make arrangements for her to be admitted tomorrow."

"Thank you. That takes a load off my mind if I don't need to worry about Edna."

"No, you won't. I'll take care of things. I'll go over now and tell her the doctor wants her back in rehab. Then go out tomorrow and take her over to the hospital. Meanwhile, you just take care of yourself. Are you getting enough sleep? Do you need anything to help you rest?"

"No thank you. I take something." He finished his drink.

"How are your boys? Do they have someone to take care of them?"

"Yes, my sister is there from Portland. She's putting the boys on a plane tomorrow morning. I'll pick them up in Colorado Springs at three o'clock."

"You take care of the boys, I'll take care of Edna." Mary stood, "Let's go back to the motel so I can get my car and I will take care of everything."

Mark put money on the table to pay for the drinks, "Mary, I can't thank you enough for what you have been doing. And taking care of getting her to rehab is just too much. Don't you work full-time at the hospital?"

"Yes, but I need to use some of the comp time I have built up and helping take care of Edna is a good use for it. Did you know she and I went through school together? She was two years ahead of me but we were friends all our adult life. Helping her is paying her and Robert back for all the kindness they have shown me over the years."

"I will accept your kindness. Thank you." They left the Wagon Wheel and went back to the motel.

On her way home, Mary debated if she should tell the Sheriff about Edna's dog. She decided she needed to call him anyway to tell him Edna would be going back to rehab.

* * *


The deputies pulled off the Forest road in behind a big F250. Ross came out of the trees to the north and hurried to meet them. "I tracked her along that north trail for about a hundred yards then recognized your truck. Let's get these horses unloaded."

The men sprung into action unloading the horses.

"Have you seen her or just horse tracks?" Warren backed the sorrel out so Darrell could unload the bay.

"Horse tracks and shoe tracks, but they're fresh. She's walking him so she shouldn't be far ahead." Darrell handed the bay over to Ross and unloaded Darrell's two horses. Randy was already on the sorrel and Ross mounted the bay. The other two deputies swung into the saddle, ready to go.

They headed the horses down the north path, "How well do you know this area?" Ross asked.

"Not as well as you do, I'm sure," Warren knew Ross worked as a hunting guide in this area. "Do you have a suggestion?"

"Yes, the trail just over there. It circles around a bit but ends up meeting this trail in about a mile and a half, maybe a little further. Why don't you and Randy take that one and Darrell and I will take the north trail? That work?" Ross glanced at the deputies nodding heads.

The group split up and walked the horses down the trails. Clark and Warren took a game trail. It was thick and hard to move through without the rider folded over the horses' neck. The men had to be careful not to be hit in the face with a branch of pine needles. They stopped every few minutes to listen for any sound of another person or horse.

Ross and Darrell followed the tracks through a wider winding path of dense pine and spruce trees stopping along the way to listen. They had stopped and Ross dismounted to check a fork in the trail to make sure they were still following the tracks. Darrell heard a horse whinny and his bay responded. Darrell put his heels into the horse's side and galloped into a small clearing where a buckskin gelding stood, munching grass.

Hearing another horse whinny, Angie jumped from her make shift lunch of potato chips and cold hot dogs. She gathered her provisions to mount her horse. Darrell caught sight of her just as she mounted.

"Angie! Hi. We've been looking for you. Are you okay?" He stopped his horse abruptly, not wanting to scare her. In a calm voice, he repeated, "Are you okay?"

Ross eased his horse into the clearing assessing the scene. Angie fumbled with plastic bags, trying to put them over the saddle horn when she saw him.

"Angie," Ross hollered.

She froze, recognizing him. "Mr. Campbell, what are you doing here?"

"Your mom is worried about you, Angie. She sent us to look for you. Aren't you ready to go home?" Ross dismounted and slowly walked towards her.

Angie tried to hurry, saying, "I'm not going back home. I hate that woman; she treats me like a baby. She even took my cell phone away so I can't call Dad. He wouldn't take my cell phone. I need to call him to come get me." She was facing the horse still struggling with the bags. She dropped one and reached into it.

"Why don't you come with us and we'll all sit down and talk to your mom?" Ross halted his steps when he realized she had drawn a Husar pistol out of the sack on the ground. Holding it in both hands, she aimed it towards the two men.

Darrell stopped dismounting and sat still.

"Hold on now, Angie. You don't want to hurt anyone. Can I have the handgun?" Ross reached out his hand but didn't move forward.

She shook her head. "No way, I'm not going back home. You just go away and leave me alone."

"Okay, Angie, we'll take you wherever you want to go. You want to go see your dad. We'll take you. Just give one of us the gun," Darrell tried to reason.

"No, go away. You'll take me back to Mom. I'm not going back there." There was a noise to her left and she turned a bit. "Stay where you are," She hollered in the direction of the sound.

The noise stopped.

Wanting her attention back to himself, Ross said, "Angie, I have a cell phone here and you can call your dad. But, my cell phone doesn't get bars up here so we'll wait until we get down to the Ranger Station. You can call your dad from there, okay?"

Ross had been told a little about what had gone on at her house the night before. He knew part of the problem centered on her not being able to spend the weekend with her father.

She was still pointing the pistol at the men, but they could tell she was considering it. "You are trying to trick me aren't you? You want me to give you this gun then you will take me back to my mother."

"Angie, where did you get the gun?" Darrell thought if she got her mind off how angry she was with her mother, she might let her guard down.

"I found it."

"Really? That is quite a thing to just find. Where did you find it?" Darrell tried to take her mind off her dilemma.

"Butter was thirsty, so we stopped down by the river so he could drink. I found it laying on the bank."

"Angie, how about if I give you my cell phone then you give me the gun? Kind of a trade? Will that work? Then we go back to the Ranger Station and you can call your dad. You will carry the phone so the first sign we have reception you can call. Okay?" Ross was used to negotiating with his daughter, Vanessa, Angie's best friend.

"Well, I don't know. I don't trust you guys."

The men could tell the eleven-year-old was considering the idea. Warren and Randy quietly stood several feet behind her.

"Angie, you trust me. You trust me when I take you and Van camping. You trust me when you spend the night with us," Ross cajoled her.

She shifted her hold on the pistol slightly. Ross held his hand out.

Just then Butter, her gelding sensed new horses in the vicinity and let out a whinny as he turned, moving his hindquarters into Angie's side, knocking her off balance. Warren saw the advantage and dove for the girl as Randy went for the gun. A shot rang out as Warren encircled Angie with his arms around her arms and chest. He lifted her off the ground and whirled her away from the other men.

Twisting her around away from the gun as it went off. Warren lost his footing, the heel of his well-worn boot banging into a rock. He landed with half his weight across Angie's stomach, knocking the breath out of her. He quickly rolled off.

"You okay, kid?" He helped her stand up and brushed her off.

She was bent over sucking in air. Gasping for breath, "No. Why did you do that? That hurt!"

"Because we don't like kids playing with guns. Especially when the guns are pointed at deputies. Are you the kid that shot at Clark earlier?" Warren didn't mean to end up on the ground on top of her but he had no patience for stubborn little girls playing with guns.

Ross used his right hand to clasp her shoulder. He turned the girl around to face him. "Are you okay, Angie?"

"No, that guy pushed me to the ground and fell on me. It hurt!" With her arms folded across her chest, her indignant look took in all the men.

"You had a handgun pointed at us. What did you think would happen?" Clark put the safety on, unloaded the gun, put the shells in his pocket and stuck the pistol in his waistband. As he turned around, he noticed blood running down Ross' hand. "You've been shot!"

Randy pushed Ross's other hand away from his arm and pulled his jacket back. The open wound on the inside of his arm below his short sleeve bled profusely. His jacket cuff was already saturated. He couldn't tell how big or deep it was with all the blood.

Angie gasped. "Oh, no. You're hurt."

Then it struck her. "Van is going to be so mad at me."

Angie stood stunned as she watched the men gather around Ross to assess his wound and try to stop the bleeding.

She panicked and ran.

At the sound of a noise behind them, the men all turned in time to spot her mount and kick Butter in the ribs to move out fast. They exchanged astonished glances and bolted into action.

Darrell and Randy ran for Butter, Warren mounted his horse. Warren skirted the men at a trot and took out across the clearing after Angie at a full gallop.

Darrell and Randy stood empty-handed shaking their heads. "Warren is always one step ahead of everyone else. Let him chase her," Darrell sighed.

"I'll take the horses back to the ranger station and make sure Ross gets to a doctor. You go help Warren." Darrell helped Ross put his jacket back on as Clark mounted and followed Warren.

The trail she took out of the clearing was a hiking trail, wider and less dense. It was easier traveling but she could hear hoof beats close behind her. Butter was not a fast horse and the moment the trail widened, Warren closed the gap between them, reached out and grabbed her horse's reins. He pulled them to a stop.

Randy was right behind them. He pulled his horse to a stop and dismounted. He pulled Angie off Butter's back and set her on the ground. "I have had enough of you for one day. Do you have any idea how much trouble you are in? You run away, you shoot at me then you shoot and wound Ross. You, young lady, don't have to worry about going home, you are spending the night in jail."

Warren held Butter's reins. "You take her horse, she's riding with me."

Randy picked Angie up, set her in the saddle and climbed up behind her.

\* \* \*

Darrell used his clean kerchief as a tourniquet to stop the bleeding in Ross' arm. It seemed to be working. Giving Ross a penetrating look, Darrell asked, "Are you going to be okay for a few minutes? I need to find the bullet that hit you. I can't go back to the office without it or I'll be out here with a flashlight tonight looking for it."

"That old Sheriff doesn't give much leeway does he?"

Darrell searched the ground as Ross looked at the nearby trees.

"No, Hobson runs a pretty tight ship. That is one of the reasons I don't mind doing this part-time."

"I think I found it." Ross gestured at a pine tree where the bark had been taken off the trunk about five feet from the ground. Darrell took his pocketknife out and whittling the bullet out.

When Darrell and Ross got to the Ranger station, they put a clean cloth on the wound. Since he had cell service, Darrell phoned the office and told Dee what happened, and that he was taking Ross to the hospital.

\* \* \*

Debbie had phoned and left three voice messages on her ex-husband's cell phone before he finally called back. "Sorry, there is no reception going over these passes and I didn't stop for coffee until just now. The messages you left just mentioned Angie. What is going on? Have they found Angie?"

"Well, they found her but she got away. Oh, heaven, Chris, Angie has a gun and shot at a deputy. The Sheriff wants to know if you still have your weapon or if she could have taken it."

"My gun? No, I checked my bag before I left this morning. It's still in there. Angie has a gun and shot at a deputy? What in the hell is going on? Shit, I'm already in the edge of Utah. I've got to deliver this load. I can't make it back before tomorrow sometime."

"The Sheriff won't let me help because she has that damn gun. He just. . . ."

"Hold on a second, I've got another call coming in." Debbie caught the click telling her she was on hold.

"Hello," Chris answered, angry at having his conversation interrupted.

"Dad!"

"Angie! Where are you?"

"I'm at the Ranger Station with Mr. Campbell and some deputies. Dad, can you come get me?"

"Honey, I'm in Utah. I'll be back tomorrow. Look, I'll take you to dinner tomorrow night, okay."

"Nooo. Dad, you don't understand! I shot Mr. Campbell! They're going to put me in jail!" Angie held Ross's phone away from her as she yelled at it. "Dad!"

He took the phone, "Chris, this is Randy Clark. Angie will be at the sheriff's office. Call Debbie and tell her to meet us there." Before Chris could ask any questions, he hung up, handed the phone back to Ross and gave the girl a look evil enough to quiet her moaning and groaning.

\* \* \*

Randy took out his cell and phoned the office. "We found Angie and are headed to town. How is Ross?" He knew Darrell would call as soon as he had cell service to let the Sheriff know what had happened.

Dee took a deep breath. "Ross is in the emergency room getting stitches and Debbie called and said she was on her way here. Have you turned that kid over your knee and spanked her yet, Randy?"

"No, but it crossed my mind about ten times. We're loading the horses and should be there within the hour. I'll run Angie by the emergency room. I don't think she's hurt badly.

But she has some scratches and in the commotion, Warren fell on top of her. Tell Debbie to meet us there."

Warren was helping the ranger put his horses back in the corral and loading the two horses Darrell had brought into the trailer. Darrell called to Warren, "Let's go."

Angie watched to make sure that her buckskin had been loaded.

Warren got in Darrell's truck and waved at Randy and the ranger as he pulled out of the drive.

Clark indicated for Angie to get in his truck and thanked the ranger for the loan of the horses. They drove in silence all the way to the edge of Cold Springs. She had her head down and would occasionally make a noise. The deputy assumed she was sobbing. "Angie, I'm taking you to the emergency room to make sure you are okay. You have scratches and Warren fell on top of you. Your mom will meet us there."

"I didn't mean to shoot Mr. Campbell. The gun just went off. Van will never forgive me for hurting her dad. She will hate me forever." Her sobbing turned into full mega crying. Randy turned on the radio and George Strait boomed over the speakers, assuring everyone that all his Exes Live in Texas.

\* \* \*

Mary Harris entered the office and stopped in front of the dispatcher's desk. "Hi, Dee, is Sheriff Hobson in?"

Hearing Mary's voice, Jim stepped out of his office and signaled Mary to come on back. "Hi, Mary, how can I help you?"

Mary entered the office and took the designated chair, saying, "Jim, you told me to see what I could find out about Joyce Hunter. Well, I talked to my friend at Gunnison Memorial and she gave me some background on the woman. She has had a hard life. She left home before finishing high school and was married a year later. That marriage didn't last but two years before her alcoholic husband filed for divorce. She remarried two years later and got pregnant with Tiffany. That marriage didn't last long, either. Most of her employment was in restaurants, bars, and nursing homes. She spent most of her adult life on and off food stamps. Surprisingly, Tiffany didn't finish high school but got her GED with the help of a teacher. Joyce and Tiffany both drive old cars that seem on their last legs. The last job Joyce had in Gunnison was working in the hospital cafeteria. She has a hard time keeping jobs. She's hard to get along with. Never likes anyone she works with and gossips a lot. Thinks the world owes her something. My friend also thinks she 'takes things that aren't hers'. I worry about Edna being safe there with her."

A memory flashed through both Mary's and the Sheriff's minds of the sociopath they got committed to a mental facility two years ago.

Hobson made a note to check with various people in Gunnison about the Hunters.

Mary continued with the information she had gathered. "This job taking care of Edna is probably the best job Joyce's had in a while. The hospital in Gunnison doesn't pay cafeteria workers very well. Why isn't she trying to do a better job? She and Tiffany have a place to stay with food and car expenses paid plus a monthly salary. That sounds a lot better than anything she has had before. I don't get it."

"Mary, some people don't realize when they have a good thing going. They think the world owes them something and the only way they know to get it is to take it."

Picking up her purse to leave, "Oh, I need to tell you, Doctor Levine is putting Edna back in the hospital for rehab tomorrow. Mark agreed it was a great idea."

"Well, good. I agree. Getting her away from the Hunter women is what she needs. I phoned Mark and asked him to come visit with me tomorrow morning. His boys are coming here in the afternoon."

"Yes, I had coffee with him earlier. Mark isn't in the best of shape. I hope the boys being here will help him cope with Caroline's death."

"He's taking it hard, isn't he?"

"Yes, he is." Mary didn't want to come right out and say it but she didn't think Mark had anything to do with Caroline's death.

* * *

Angie and Randy met Debbie as they entered the emergency room. She ran to her daughter, put her arms around her and gave her a big hug. Pushing Angie back at arm's length and looking her over, Debbie noticed she had a scrape on the side of her face. Her clothes were dirty and her eyes were red and swollen from crying.

"Angie, are you okay? Are you hurt?" Debbie glanced over at Randy.

"She has some scrapes from riding through the trees and brush. When we took the weapon away from her, Darrell and she fell to the ground. Darrell landed on top of her. I want to make sure she doesn't have any serious injuries."

The nurse at the desk handed Debbie forms to fill out and led her and Angie back to an exam area. She gave Angie a hospital gown to put on. They could hear people in the next area and Angie recognized Ross' voice.

Leaning over to whisper in her mother's ear, "Mom, I shot Mr. Campbell. I didn't mean to. The deputy grabbed the gun, and it just went off. I'm so sorry. I'm so sorry." She sobbed again.

Putting her arms around Angie's shoulders, "I know, honey, we will straighten this out later. Now, does any place hurt?"

Debbie felt her arms as she helped her out of her clothes and into the gown.

Through tears, Angie said, "Only my hip. I think it's bruised. That man, Warren, fell on me."

As Dr. Levine pulled back the curtain, "I hear you've had a busy day, young lady." The doctor pulled the stethoscope from around his neck and listened to Angie's lungs and heart. Examining her arms, "Debbie, how are you doing?"

"I've been better. Doctor Levine, how is Ross? Mr. Campbell?" Debbie straightened the sheet over her daughter's legs.

"Ten stitches and a tetanus shot. He had more stitches than that when a roll of barbed wire he was stretching snapped back on his arm last summer." Smiling, the doctor added, "He's one of my more experienced patients."

"You know I didn't mean to hurt Mr. Campbell. I just feel terrible. Van will really be angry. She might never speak to me again," Angie lamented, as her limbs were being stretched and probed by the doctor.

"She mentioned her hip hurt." Debbie pulled the sheet up and motioned for her to show the doctor where it hurt.

After looking at the bruise on her hip and finishing the exam, Doctor Levine gave his opinion, "Well, Angie, I think you are none the worse for wear." He turned to Debbie, "She has scratches and bruises. When the deputy fell on her, he knocked the wind out of her. She's fine."

The doctor helped Angie off the table. "Now young lady, it's time for you to face all those people I saw in the waiting room as I came in."

When the ladies entered the waiting room the only one waiting for them was the deputy. Ross and the rest of the Campbell family had left. "Are you ready to go talk to the Sheriff?" Randy crossed his arms and cocked his head at Angie.

"Yeah, I guess." She resigned herself to the inevitable as her mother nodded her head.

\* \* \*

Sitting at the table in the sheriff's break room, Randy offered the ladies drinks. Angie sat quietly beside her mother and played with her can of Diet Coke. Both Debbie and her daughter worried how much trouble Angie had gotten herself into. Debbie knew things would work out but Angie's mind was working overtime. *Mom and Dad wouldn't let them put me in jail, would they? I bet Van hates me for shooting her dad. Will she ever speak to me again? If I go to jail will I have to quit school? I like the school here.*

Sheriff Hobson came into the room and sat in the chair across from Angie. He placed a small black tape recorder on the table between them.

Her eyes got big. She stared at her mother.

Debbie took a deep breath, "Do we need a lawyer?"

"You have that right, any time you want it. I just want to ask Angie some questions. Mostly about where she got that gun." Hobson waited for Debbie to respond. She took a few seconds to look at her daughter then nodded at the Sheriff.

"Okay," Hobson spoke the pertinent information into the recorder as Randy sat down beside him.

"Angie, it is my understanding from your mom that you and she had an argument last night. When she woke up this morning, you were not in bed or anywhere on the property where you live. Angie, is this true?"

She nodded as she played with her drink.

"I'm sorry, Angie. You have to answer with a yes or no," The Sheriff instructed.

She responded with a very shaky "Yes".

"You live on the ranch with your mom and your aunt and uncle. Is that right?"

"Yes."

"You had an argument with your mother

and that upset you, right?"

"Yes."

"Then what happened, Angie?" Hobson leaned back in his chair.

"My mom always treats me like a baby. She won't let me do anything. She even took my phone," Angie stated through gritted teeth looking at her lap.

"Angie, we don't care what the argument was about. That is between you and your mom. We will assume that you felt you had a reason to leave. Okay?"

"Okay." She stared at the heavy-set man across from her and wandered why he was not giving her a lecture on running away from home. This threw her off guard and helped her relax. *Maybe he isn't taking Mom's side.*

"Now, after the argument what did you do?"

"I waited until everyone went to bed and they were asleep then I got my sleeping bag and some food. I saddled my horse and walked it out of the pen and a little way down the drive. Then I kept going."

"Where were you going?"

"I just wanted to be by myself and away from Mom." Angie didn't look at her mother, only at the lawman. "I know where there are some nice camping areas in the National Forest so I went there until I could call my dad and go stay with him."

"Okay, which road did you take to the forest?"

"I took our drive to the paved road. I guess it's a county road. Then around town and over to the picnic area where the creek is."

"Angie, how did you find the gun?"

"Oh, well, when I got to the bridge on the paved road. You know by the river before you get to the picnic area? I was thirsty, and I thought Butter might be, too, so I stopped and walked around the bridge to the river so he could drink. I sat down and rested a while. I laid my sleeping bag out under some bushes where it was dry. I think I fell asleep. The sun wasn't up but I wanted to get to the campground. When I went to get back on Butter, I heard him kick something. I looked down and there was that gun."

"Did you see anyone around as you stopped by the bridge? Any cars or anyone on foot?"

"No. I wouldn't have stopped if I had seen anyone."

"Did you notice any cars at all when you were on the paved road?"

"Well, I saw a couple of cars when I went around town but that was all. When I stopped at the bridge, I could see the red tail lights of a car real far up the road. But, there weren't any other cars."

"Could you tell if the vehicle with the tail

lights was a car or truck?"

"Nooo." Angie gave the Sheriff a look saying the question was stupid.

"When you saw the gun, did you pick it up? What did you do with it?"

"I picked it up and put it in the bag with the potato chips."

Debbie's hands held her face as she braced her elbows on the table and cringed at her daughter's answers.

"Angie, have you ever been around guns much? Have you ever shot a gun?"

Debbie could no longer be silent. "She's not allowed around guns or to shoot one."

"Mom is right. She won't even let my dad show me his gun. My uncle's rifles are all locked up in a case under his bed. It's too heavy for me to pull out." The last sentence was not supposed to come out. Angie's eyes flew wide open and she peered at her mother like she had just confessed to a heinous crime.

Debbie opened her mouth, but the Sheriff shook his head to warn her not to interrupt him. "So, even though you had never handled a gun, you decided to take this one along with you?"

"Yes, I thought I might need it for bears or something."

"Or deputies." Randy murmured under his breath, his anger still smoldering.

Hobson gave his deputy a quick glance. "Okay, you found the handgun on the ground by the bridge and decided to take it. Then where did you go?"

"I stopped at the picnic area and tied my horse, Butter, behind the bushes and ate. Then I heard a truck and ran to Butter to try to make him be quiet. The truck pulled in. I think it was him." Angie indicated Randy. "He hollered at me. I tried to hang the bags back on the saddle when the gun fell out. It went off as I picked it up. It scared Butter, and he took off. I went after him."

"Were you holding the pistol when it fired?"

She hesitated a minute, "Yeah, I guess. I picked it up off the ground. I had it in my hand as I chased Butter. I remember that because it was heavy. Butter is hard to catch with just one hand."

The young girl answered all of their questions but couldn't add anything else about the gun. "One more thing, Angie, I want you and your mom to ride out to the bridge and show Randy exactly where you found the gun. Okay?"

"Now?" Debbie was exhausted both physically and mentally.

"Please? It would help us if we could take care of all the little details as soon as possible."

"Okay, Sheriff. Come on, Angie." Debbie ushered her out the door followed by Randy.

"One more thing before you go. I need a

set of her fingerprints." Randy waited, watching Angie's fear as she turned and faced her mother.

Nodding her head in understanding, Debbie said, "Let's do it now, so we can go home."

The girl recoiled. "But Mom!"

"You are not under arrest, Angie." The deputy assured her as he led her to his office where he kept his supplies. "I need your prints so when the techs lift prints off the gun, they know which ones are yours. Okay?"

When they finished with the fingerprints, Randy gestured at the door, "Okay, Angie, let's go look at where you found the gun. We will take my car."

He led them out of the office.

* * *

"No, the other side of the bridge." Angie pointed up the road as she leaned over the front seat of the cruiser. Debbie and Angie got out and stood by the car.

Randy parked on the side of the road. He asked Angie and Debbie to stay on the pavement and for Angie to just point to the place and give him directions when he got close.

He inched his way down the bank keeping a sharp eye out for any tracks on the leaf-laden grass. The cottonwoods that shaded the riverbank had distributed a vast amount of leaves last fall and made for a slippery descent. As he got closer to the bridge, he saw horse and small shoe prints and snapped photos. He spied a small patch of cleared ground where the damp earth showed through the leaves.

Angie shouted from above, "Right there! Where the leaves are pushed away. When I found the gun, I wanted to see if there was anything else there and I moved the leaves."

The deputy snapped more photos from various directions then rummaged around the area looking for any other evidence. He walked back up the bank and found an empty cartridge, which hadn't made it as far down the bank as the gun. He used a plastic evidence bag to pick it up. After searching, he found a second one and added it to the bag. More photos, then he climbed up the bank and stood beside Angie and Debbie.

"Anything else you remember when you found the gun?"

"No. I led Butter down the bank over there where it isn't so steep." She pointed to a place about ten yards away. "Then I walked him up by the bridge so he could get a drink. It was still dark. I wouldn't have seen the gun without my flashlight."

"You didn't see any cars or people around?" Randy gave it another try.

"No."

"Okay, Let's go back to the office." He

held the car door open for the ladies.

Back at the office, he reminded her and her mother they would need to come in tomorrow and sign the statement Angie had given.

# CHAPTER 7

"Thank you for coming in, Mark. I need to ask you several questions. Please don't take offense. They're pretty routine." The Sheriff said early the next morning as Mark sat in the office with a cup of coffee. Hobson turned on the tape recorder and stated the pertinent information to start the interview.

Hobson took out a notepad. "How was your marriage? Any problems?"

Hesitating and then clearing his throat, "Well, . . . over the years, everyone has problems. I guess, recently the only thing was Edna's illness and Caroline having to run back and forth to Cold Springs."

"Did Caroline like Seattle?" He read from his notes in front of him.

"She wasn't crazy about leaving Colorado but I couldn't turn down the job offer. I think she was okay with it until Edna had to have the operation; then it got kind of bad. She hated to be away from the boys but she knew that Edna was depending on her, too."

"How about your relationship?" Hobson didn't want to lead with specific questions so he kept it general.

"I've been working late and haven't had much time for her and the boys. We have quarreled over her trips to Edna's." Mark stared down concentrating on his coffee cup.

"You don't feel your marriage was in any trouble?"

Confused, Mark looked up, "No. Did someone tell you it was?"

"Like I said, these are just routine questions." Then, changing the topic, "Mark, do you own a gun?"

"No. Absolutely not. Caroline hated guns. Didn't want one in the house. I gave my hunting rifle to my brother after we got married. That was the only gun I ever owned."

"Are you aware of any problem Caroline had with anyone here in Cold Springs?"

"Only problem I know of is this thing that's going on with Edna and Joyce Hunter. I'm not sure what all that is about. I guess Mary Harris and Sarah Howard told Caroline they thought Joyce might be taking advantage or even abusing her. That's why she jumped on a plane for Colorado."

"How about someone from Caroline's past that may hold a grudge?" The Sheriff was grasping at straws and he knew it.

Shaking his head in thought, Mark replied, "I can't think of anything. Edna might remember something."

He stood and offered his hand to Mark. "Thanks for taking the time to come in and talk to me. We're doing everything we can to find the person who killed Caroline."

"Yeah, I know." Mark shook hands with Hobson and walked out with the slumped shoulders of the grief-stricken.

Hobson wished he could do more to comfort the husband. His gut told him Mark had nothing to do with her death. He sat pondering the interview.

"Phone call on line two. Some rancher is missing a horse." Dee called from her desk.

"Jim Hobson."

"Hi, Jim. This is Cary, Joe McCall's daughter. Dad is missing a horse, a sorrel mare. She was in a locked pasture and she's not there now. So, I guess she was stolen?" the soft voice on the other end of the line explained.

"Well, Cary, Joe's horse is at Dave Watson's place on the north side of town, Watson Cattle Company. Let me give you Dave's phone number. She's over eating Dave's hay." Hobson flipped through the papers on his desk and read the number to Larson.

"Oh, boy. I bet Dave is mad. His fresh cut hay?"

"Yep, but it's already baled."

"Oh, no. Thanks, I'll call him. How did she get over there?"

He let out a sigh, "That we don't know. We just got a call from Dave saying he had an extra horse in his pasture. Cary, I need you or Joe to come and file a report and explain the circumstances. Whenever is convenient."

"Circumstances? I don't know any circumstances. She just isn't in her pasture where I left her. I'll be in sometime today to talk to you about it. Thanks, Sheriff."

Hanging up the phone, he tried to figure out a logical reason someone would move a horse from one pasture to another about eight miles away. It was not April fool's day, Halloween, or any high school or 4-H celebration. And, the horse was not looking for 'greener pastures' on her own.

Not able to spend any more time with a theft that had been partly solved, he grabbed his hat off the rack and walked by Dee's desk. "I'll be out at Edna Bristol's place. I'll be back after lunch."

\* \* \*

Debbie and Angie found Randy in his office waiting for them. After being seated, he handed Debbie two sheets of paper stating the information that Angie had given to the Sheriff yesterday. Angie read it looking over Debbie's shoulder. When they were finished, both agreed that it was correct, and both signed at the bottom.

"Angie, why don't you go out and wait in the car for me, okay?" Her mother asked.

When she had left the office, Debbie turned to Randy. "What will happen to Angie?

Do you know?"

"No, I don't. The Sheriff will talk to the DA and see if he wants to charge her with anything. I don't think Ross will want her charged. He insisted at the hospital that it was just an accident."

"Okay, thanks, Randy. What about your truck? Well, I guess it belongs to the county?"

"That's up to the Sheriff and the DA."

Debbie nodded and left.

\* \* \*

*Perfect timing.* The Sheriff thought as he pulled his SUV up beside Mary's car. Mary had just helped Edna into her Toyota and stopped to speak with him.

"Good morning. I am just taking Edna back to rehab," Mary remarked as she put the suitcase in the back seat.

"Morning. I don't want to keep you. How is Edna doing?" He waved at her through the car window.

"She's doing fine."

Edna rolled down the window to say, "I'm doing just fine, Sheriff. Do you need to talk to me?"

"No, you go on. I'll just say 'hi' to Joyce." Hobson waited as they drove onto the street and down the block. He walked up the steps and knocked on the door.

The door swung open and a young, rather plump woman in tight jeans with a bridle in her hand stared at him.

"Hi, I'm Sheriff Hobson, is Joyce Hunter here?"

The girl's face remained expressionless as she hollered, "Mom, there's a cop here to see you." With that, she pushed past Jim and went to her car leaving the front door to the house open.

"What?" Joyce appeared in the doorway wearing what Hobson thought was either a housedress or a Mumu. He remembered his wife trying to explain the difference to him one day. He thought it resembled an extremely bright red and yellow tent.

"Hi, I'm Sheriff Hobson. I'd like to talk to you a few minutes. Can I come in?"

Joyce continued to stare at him.

"Can I come in?"

Glancing down the street, she said, "Edna just left."

"Yes, I came to talk to you."

"What do you want?"

"Well, if we are going to visit out here on the steps with the neighbors watching, I guess that is okay." He took a small notebook and pen out of his jacket pocket. "Where were you the night Caroline Archer was killed? That would have been . . ."

"Get in here! I don't want the nosey

neighbors to see you!" Joyce stepped back to let him in the house. She walked through the hall into the living room and flopped down in the recliner. The Sheriff noticed the end table next to her chair held the remains of her breakfast. He followed and sat on the end of the couch. "Now, where were you the night Caroline Archer was killed?"

"Right here taking care of Edna. As always." She sniffed.

"All evening?" He pulled a notepad and pen out of his pocket.

"Yes, all evening. Where do you think I would be in this poor-excuse for a town?"

He nodded. "Did you make any phone calls to Caroline that night?"

"Why would I call her? I don't even know her phone number."

"You don't have her number for emergency purposes? What happens if Edna gets sick?"

Joyce frowned. "Oh, I guess it's programed into Edna's phone. I would just dial two when I need her but I have never had to call her. And, I didn't call her that night."

Looking at his notes, "Was your daughter, Tiffany, here with you? That was three nights ago."

He watched Joyce hesitate before she responded. "Yeah, she was here."

"All evening?"

"I don't remember. Probably not, she likes to go out and visit with her friends most evenings."

"She hasn't lived here long, but she has a lot of friends?" He found that hard to believe since he thought Tiffany was shy.

"She makes friends easy. Especially men friends." She snorted looking towards the kitchen.

"Do you remember what time she left that night and about what time she got back?"

"No!"

"Did Caroline call you to tell you she was coming to visit?"

"No."

"Did she call Edna?"

Joyce shook her head, "I don't remember. There is an extension phone in her room. She answers it herself."

"You didn't talk to Caroline the night she was killed or the day before?"

"No. What? You think I killed her?" Joyce jumped up, went to the front door and opened it wide. "Get out. Get out. You can't question me like this without a lawyer." All of a sudden she was very upset, red in the face and shaking.

Realizing he was being thrown out, he got up and went to the door. "Thank you for your time. And, just to let you know, this conversation isn't over."

The door slammed behind him as he

walked to the county's black SUV.

* * *

Randy tossed the plastic bag with the bullet that shot Ross Campbell on the Sheriff's desk beside the one taken from Caroline. He then placed the larger bag holding the Harus pistol taken from Angie Hudson beside them. Sitting down in the chair in front of Hobson's desk, he said, "The handgun is registered to Travis Bristol."

Hobson's eyebrows shot up. "Really? Edna's nephew?"

"Yep." Randy scooted forward in his chair ready to leave.

Looking at his watch, Hobson stood. "He still works at the lumberyard?"

"I saw him there yesterday." Clark put his hat on.

"Let's go."

The men almost hit Dee coming out of the break room.

"Going somewhere?" she called to the closing door.

"Be right back." The deputy yelled as the door banged shut.

The cruiser made the eight blocks in a matter of minutes. The lawmen found Travis Bristol beside the lumberyard shed helping a guy load 2x4s in his pickup.

Hobson called to him, "Travis, can we talk to you when you're through?"

"Sure thing, Sheriff." He tied red flagging to the lumber sticking out of the back of the pickup and waved at the driver as he pulled away.

Smiling, he walked over to the two men. He was a lean, dark-haired man in his middle thirties. He took off his ball cap and wiped his sweaty forehead with his arm. "What can I do for you? Did the jail fall down and you need lumber to rebuild?" he joked.

"No, Travis, we would like you to come down to the Sheriff's office and talk about the Harus handgun that's registered in your name." Hobson watched closely for Travis's reaction while the deputy edged to the side between Travis and the parking lot.

"My gun? What about it?" His brows closed together over his eyes.

"Do you have it with you? Can I see it?" Hobson waited.

Still frowning at the lawmen, "It's in my pickup. Under the seat. This way." Travis headed across the parking lot where seven various colors and models of pickups sat. He led them to a brown single-cab Dodge and opened the door. He felt under the seat, opened the door wider and reached further under. Looking confused he turned to the Sheriff, "Maybe it got shoved to the other side." Travis walked around and opened the passenger side and searched under the seat, pulling out various rags and tools. His head was on the cab floor as he tried to look under the seat.

"Shit, it's not here." He rose up and looked the lawman in the eyes. "Okay, it's time to tell me what this is about."

"Travis, there is a Harus handgun laying on my desk at the office. Let's go see if you recognize it." The Sheriff waited for Travis' answer.

Still bewildered, Travis nodded to his truck. "Can I drive my truck over?"

Randy and Travis both watched Hobson nod. "Go tell Lacey you're taking your lunch break and meet us at my office."

The lawmen were waiting when Travis entered the office.

Travis had a panicked expression. "What is this all about? I thought my gun was still in my truck but you say you have it? What's going on?"

Hobson signaled for him to sit down. He had taken the pistol out of the bag and wiped the black fingerprint dust off. Fingerprints had been removed earlier. The Sheriff pushed the handgun over to Travis, who picked it up and turned it around twice.

"Yeah, I'm sure this is my gun. Where is the holster? I own a side holster I keep it in." He waited patiently for one of the men to explain why they had his gun.

"A young lady found your pistol along the river bank just outside the National park. Any idea how it got there? When was the last time you saw it?"

"I thought about that on the way over here. The last time I remember having it was last Wednesday night. I put a bottle of Jack Daniels under the seat and remembered bumping the gun. I don't know anything about it being over by the river. No idea how it got there. Or, when it was taken." Travis shook his head.

"I'm careful about keeping track of it. I always keep the safety on and keep it in a holster. I keep it in the truck because my wife doesn't like a handgun in the house. My hunting rifle and shotgun she allows in the house because they're kept in the gun safe. But, she makes me keep the handgun in my truck." He knew he was not making much sense but every thought that came into his head just blurted right out his mouth.

Randy entered the conversation, "I noticed when you went to your truck to look for the weapon you didn't unlock the door. Do you ordinarily keep your truck doors unlocked?"

"Yeah, bad habit, I know. I've just lived in the country too much. I actually have to remember to lock the truck doors." A guilty look crossed his face.

"Who knew you kept a gun in your

truck?" The Sheriff waited for an answer.

"Me, my wife, my brother-in-law, a couple of friends I go hunting with. The bouncer at Kelly's; he borrowed it one night. The minister at the Baptist Church, I had to kill a snake for him last spring. Those are all I can remember. I've had that thing for three years."

"Okay." The Sheriff surmised. "I assume that half the town knows you carry a handgun in your truck. Right?"

With a hangdog look, Travis admitted, "Yeah, probably." Then, taking a deep breath, "How did you get it? Some young lady found it?"

Randy kept quiet and let Hobson tell Travis what he wanted him to know. "Well, she found the gun and decided to use it a couple of times, too."

"Oh, god, no. Did she kill someone?" Travis' worst fears surfaced.

"No, she shot at Randy's truck and put a dent in the top. Then she used it to take a piece out of Ross Campbell's arm before my deputies took it away from her."

Travis shook his head in disbelief. Hobson could see Travis mentally kicked himself for not keeping the gun hidden better. "When I purchased the weapon the guy at the shop asked if I wanted a metal lock box to put it in. But, I turned him down, not wanting the extra expense."

"If you can think of anyone else who knew the gun was there, let us know." Randy reminded Travis as he left.

"Do you believe him?"

"Yeah, I do." The Sheriff pushed the handgun and both bullets over to Randy. "Send Travis' pistol and the bullet that hit Ross to ballistics at the state. Make sure the bullet came from that gun. I haven't decided what to do with Angie yet. Send the bullet that killed Caroline too and see what they can tell us about it. It is the same caliber."

"Do you want me to do anything with the bullet from Kelly's robbery? I've been staring at these three bullets for an hour with that high-powered magnifying glass from the forensic kit. I swear they all look the same."

"What do you mean? They look like the same caliber but what else? Show me."

With the magnifying glass, Randy pointed out the one long mark halfway down the bullet. That one deep mark appeared the same on each one. They couldn't tell if anything else matched. The bullet taken out of the tree when Ross was shot had been flattened some on the end. The Sheriff sat, staring at the bullets then he leaned back in his chair, thinking.

"Well?" Clark picked up the three bags with the bullets and the one with the cartridges waiting for the answer.

"Oh, hell, send it too. You never know."

* * *

Later, Randy went into the sheriff's private office and folded himself onto the visitor's chair. "I talked to Angie's teachers and principal."

Taking his attention away from the papers he worked on, Hobson gave Clark his undivided attention.

"They all say she's a good kid. A little emotional at times but she's an 'A' student. Hasn't missed a day of school since she started a year ago last fall. She's on the honor roll. Plays clarinet in the band. Not the best player but she tries. When I went to their house to talk to Debbie, Angie went into a crying thing. She still feels bad about hurting Ross. He phoned her and assured he it was an accident, but it didn't help her conscience much."

The Sheriff nodded. "I haven't talked to the DA yet. Okay, she owes for the damage to your pickup, I'll see if Ross wants to press charges or the DA does. Any other property damage?"

"Cost of us going out to find her?"

"Yeah, there's that too. Let me talk to Ross and then the DA." This was one of the things Hobson hated: dealing with kids who didn't think about the problems they could cause before they made what they thought was a simple decision.

# CHAPTER 8

Kelly tipped his ball cap to Dee as he walked into the office at ten o'clock the next morning. "Morning. Is there any information on my robbery? Or, should I write it off on my income tax?"

Hobson walked out of his office. "What are you griping about, Kelly?"

"Have you found the guy that robbed me?"

"Can you give a better description than what you gave the other day?"

"Well, maybe."

"Let's hear it." The Sheriff led Kelly back to his office.

He lowered himself into a guest chair, "It isn't about the robber. It's about the car he drove. Arnold and I got to talking about his needing his truck muffler replaced, and I remembered that the car that pulled away after the robbery had a muffler problem. Not a bad one, just a little rumble, like it was loose?"

"Okay, I'll add that to the vague description you gave me. Randy can ask both car repair places if they've replaced any mufflers in the last few days. So, we're looking for an older car. Anything else you can remember?"

"No, I'm afraid not." Kelly got up.

"Kelly, do you know Tiffany Hunter?" Hobson's thoughts were pulled back to

Caroline's murder.

"Now Sheriff, if she's telling you I serve her liquor, she's lyin'. We only served her that one time before I took her false ID away. Honest, I wasn't aware she was underage until Travis Bristol told me."

Hobson's curiosity got the best of him. "How does Travis know how old Tiffany is?"

"Tiffany hangs out with his little brother and his cousin, Mandy. She likes to ride their horses. Mandy is a senior in high school and thinks it's great that someone as old as Tiffany wants to hang out and ride horses with her."

"How do you know so much about the Bristols?"

"Travis' little brother -- I guess I should call him his younger brother, he turned twenty-one last December. Anyway, Brandon comes into the bar about every other day for a hamburger and beer before he goes back to feed the horses. His father put him managing the boarding horse part of the Bristol Ranch. He gets there about four o'clock when we aren't busy and we visit. He tells me all the family problems."

"So tell me about Tiffany."

"She's man crazy, horse crazy and is a bad influence on Mandy. She's also broke most of the time. Bums money off Mandy and tries to get money off Brandon, too. He doesn't like her."

"Does she come into your place a lot?"

Kelly shook his head, "Not much. Arnold won't let her in much since we found out about the fake ID. But, if she comes in before eight, he lets her eat as long as she doesn't cause trouble or try to drink alcohol. She usually comes in with Mandy. They like our chiliburgers. I think Arnold likes those two even if they give him a problem once in awhile. He looks out for them. He makes sure some drunk doesn't pick them up. But, Arnold looks out after most of the women who come into the bar."

"What do you know about the rest of the Bristol family?"

"Sheriff, I'm a bar owner. My customers will quit coming to my place if they find out I talk to you," Kelly complained.

"I wouldn't be asking you these questions if Edna Bristol's daughter hadn't been murdered."

"Yeah, you're right. What do you want to know about them?"

"Did you know Caroline?"

"I don't remember seeing her in several years. I wasn't actually acquainted with her. Oh, I would recognize her if I saw her. That's about it."

"How about Edna?"

"Mrs. Bristol used to come in with Mrs. Dawson in the afternoon. It's quiet then and they like my chili. I haven't seen either of them since she had her operation."

"Okay, tell me what you know about Travis."

"What do I know about Travis? More than I want to." He took a deep breath and listed the facts. "He loves his wife and kids. Always carries their photos around with him. He works at the lumberyard. He doesn't like his job. Travis thinks his boss is a 'dumb ass'. He didn't get a raise like they promised him. They told him it was a bad winter, and the profits were down. He is still a little angry that Edna didn't trust him to run the hardware store after her husband died." He took another breath to continue, but the Sheriff interrupted him.

"What? He wanted to run the store after Mrs. Bristol's husband died?"

"Yeah, it seems she gave the assistant manager, Glen, a five-year lease with an option to buy. I think the lease should be up in the next few months. Anyway, Travis wanted Edna to give him that deal, but she told him Glen was older and had more experience. Glen also had money to put down to secure the option. Anyway, Travis still grumbles about it after a few beers."

The Sheriff nodded as he mentally made plans for his next visit with Edna. "Does he drink much?"

"Not usually. Not one of my more profitable customers."

"What's your information on Glen that is leasing the hardware store?"

"Very little. The only time I see him is when I go there. I don't think he drinks much and I don't recall his ever being in my bar."

"Any idea how the hardware store is doing?"

"Well now, this is pure speculation on my part. I'm not sure he is doing too well. I heard complaints when he went up on his prices. I know he lost a couple of accounts because he demanded payment in twenty days instead of the usual thirty. However, his wife is driving a new Ford." Kelly shrugged his shoulders.

"Thanks, I appreciate your help and we are working on the robbery." It was not really a lie, the Sheriff thought about it a lot, but he didn't have any leads.

As Kelly was leaving his office, Hobson grabbed his hat and told Dee he would be gone most of the day.

\* \* \*

As the Sheriff pulled his cruiser up in front of Edna's house he noted a dark green Chevy Cobalt parked in the driveway. He knocked on the door and asked for Joyce. Tiffany said she was at the store.

"Okay, I can talk to her later. Can I come in and talk to you now?" Hobson took off his hat and stepped forward. Tiffany hesitated at first but opened the door wider and led him into the living room.

She plunked herself down on the couch and nodded for him to take a chair. "Why you want to talk to me? I don't know anything about Caroline and I hardly ever see Edna. She stays in her room."

"But, you live here. Right?"

"Yeah, Edna said it was okay. I got laid off from my job in Gunnison and needed a place to stay. I've been looking for a job here." She played with the hem of her sweater and looking everywhere but at the Sheriff.

"That must be hard. There aren't too many jobs available here in Cold Springs," he sympathized. "Were you here at the house last Saturday evening?"

"I was out with friends. I didn't get home 'til late, I ran out of gas."

He pulled out a notepad and pen. "Where did you and your friends go?"

"Well, I had been over at Mandy Bristol's riding horses all afternoon. Her mom invited me to stay for dinner. After that, Mandy and I went for a ride."

"You like horses?" He tried for a subject she felt comfortable with.

"Oh, yes. Mandy owns two horses and she let's me ride any time I can."

"After dinner you went for a ride.

Horseback riding again?"

Tiffany got comfortable answering his questions. "No, Silly, it was dark. We went in my car."

"Okay, where did you and Mandy go in your car?"

She squirmed a little. He could see her anxiety level heighten. "We went to Kelly's. Arnold lets us in to eat and dance. I'm twenty-one and as long as Mandy doesn't drink, she can stay and dance too. We are kind of friends with Arnold. He makes us leave sometimes, but he's not mean about it."

"You're twenty-one, okay. How long did you stay at Kelly's?"

She let out a disgusted sigh. "Mandy had to be home by eleven so we left about ten-thirty. I dropped her off and headed for home then I ran out of gas. I had to walk home."

"Why did you walk home? Why didn't you call your mother to pick you up?"

"I phoned, but she didn't answer." The floor became her focal point for the rest of the conversation.

"You called? Did you call her cell phone?"

"She can't afford a cell phone. I called the house."

"And, she didn't answer. Does she normally answer the phone?"

"It depends on what mood she's in."

Tiffany was sure that her mother wasn't home that night but didn't want anyone to find out she might have left Edna there by herself. "Sometimes when she's watching a program on television and doesn't want to be interrupted, she lets the phone ring."

"Okay. What time did you get home?"

Tiffany bit her nails. "I'm not sure. It must have been after midnight. It was a long walk."

The Sheriff flipped the page of his notepad. "Where did you run out of gas?"

"I think its road 832. It was out close to the entrance to the National Forest. She was learning her way around the county but didn't pay much attention to the road numbers.

He frowned at her. "Yeah, I'm aware where that's at. That is quite a ways from where Mandy lives."

"I just drove around. I didn't feel like going home so early." The thread she was pulling on her sweater was getting longer.

"You didn't happen to see Caroline while you were driving around, did you. I heard she stopped at the Stop 'N Go."

Tiffany's eyes got big, and she hesitated. "No, I didn't go near that end of town. I didn't see anyone. Not Caroline or anyone else."

"So, you would recognize Caroline if you saw her?"

Tiffany nodded her head. "Yeah. She was here when I helped Mom move in. I met her."

"You didn't happen to call her that day did you?"

"No. No, why would I call her?" She got defensive.

"Did you know how to reach Caroline in case of an emergency?"

Without hesitation, "Yeah, it's number two on Edna's phone. But I've never called it."

The Sheriff stood, "Well, thank you for talking to me. If I have more questions, I'll be back. Oh, do you know when your mom will be back?" Tiffany shook her head still sitting on the couch. She made no effort to show the man out.

When he got back to his county car and started the engine, he realized that a lot of people in town were out running around that night. That didn't help his investigation any.

\* \* \*

Hobson's next stop was the rehab part of the hospital where Edna was staying. The police had two designated parking places in the doctors parking area. The Sheriff used it for this convenience but this time it meant he had to walk through the hospital to find the rehab area.

Entering the hospital, he met Mark and two boys standing at the visitor's desk with Sarah Howard and stopped.

"Hi, Mark. These young men must be your two boys." Hobson greeted Mark with a handshake.

"Yes, this is Todd and Ben. Boys, this is Sheriff Hobson. They got in this morning and we have been to visit Edna. She was real glad to see them."

Both boys stuck their hand out to shake with the Sheriff.

"Glad to meet two such nice young men. I'm sorry about your mother. You boys take care."

Both boys hung their heads and nodded.

Hobson nodded to Mark. "I need to run. I want to talk to Edna before they deliver her lunch." He continued down the long hall to rehab.

Sticking his head around the door of Edna's room, he called, "Hi, are you busy?"

"Yes, Jim, I'm busy running laps around the room." She hollered from one of the two chairs beside her bed.

"Well, I wouldn't want to interrupt that." The Sheriff sat down in the other chair and laid his wide-brimmed hat on the floor. "Mind if I ask you a few questions?"

"I know you need to, so go ahead."

"Tell me about Travis Bristol. He used to work at the hardware store?"

"Yes, he's my husband's nephew. He worked summers for us when he was in eighth grade. He worked part time all through high school, then he went away to college for a couple of years. After Robert died, I decided I didn't want to run the store anymore, so I sold Glen a five-year lease with an option to buy it. He had been our general manager for about four years and I felt he knew enough about the business he could make a go of it."

The Sheriff nodded. "How did Travis feel about that?"

"Oh, well, he didn't like it at all. He thought I should have given him the option since he was family and he had two years of business college. I sympathized with Travis but he was young. I had talked it over with Caroline and she agreed that Glen was the best bet for running the store. And we didn't think Travis could come up with any money to buy the option. Caroline was a fine businesswoman and insisted that whoever wanted the store had to be able to put money up front. They had to have a reason to make a go of it. He needed 'skin in the game' was the expression she used. Caroline could be real stubborn when it came to business."

"Is Travis still angry about not getting the option to buy?"

Edna sat with her head down, thinking, "I'm not sure you could call it angry. He did come by the house a couple of weeks ago. He said he dropped in to see how I was doing but he asked me when the option was up and if Glen was intending to buy the store. I told him the option had three more months and Glen hadn't mentioned to me one way or the other. He's been keeping up with the lease payments, but that is all I know. A couple of people told me Glen has gone up on all the prices and I think he has lost some customers because of that. But, it's not my place to say anything."

"Okay. Edna, what happened last Saturday? Before we came to tell you about Caroline. Did you make any phone calls to Caroline's cell?"

Taking a deep breath, she said, "No, I didn't call Caroline. She phoned me early that morning and told me she was coming for a visit. I figured she would be in late that night. She never likes me to wait up for her. She's always dog-tired when she gets here and wants to go right to bed. Which is okay with me. It's hard to have a serious conversation with her when she's tried. She gets very irritable."

"Okay, tell me what happened that day." The Sheriff removed a notepad from his shirt pocket along with a pen.

"Well, I don't remember anything out of the ordinary. Joyce brought me a tray for supper. I don't think Tiffany was there. I watched a little television." Edna paused and frowned. "Joyce did come in early, about eight-thirty and gave me my pain pill and the other one that is supposed to help me sleep. She said she was going to watch a movie and didn't want to be interrupted. I got drowsy and turned off the TV and went to sleep. The next thing I knew, you and Mary came to tell me about Caroline." Tears filled her eyes, and she reached for a tissue on the nightstand.

"You didn't hear doors open or close? Could Joyce have left without your knowing?"

"Well, she could have but she's not supposed to leave me alone, especially at night. Caroline pays her well for taking care of me."

"Did she ever leave you alone at night? I mean, that you are aware of."

"Jim, I've always been a sound sleeper and those pain pills along with the sleep aids Joyce insists I take really knock me out. Some nights they could move the entire house without my knowing."

"Okay, that is what I needed to know." The Sheriff turned towards the noise at the door as a nurse brought in a lunch tray. "That is my cue to leave. You take care, Edna, and mind the nurses."

\* \* \*

Hobson was in his office staring at the whiteboard when Randy found him. "How are you coming on the murder investigation?" The deputy sat down and helped the Sheriff stare at the board.

Caroline phoned Edna to tell her she was

coming.

Saturday:

10:30 Caroline called and talked to her mother.

10:50 Left Seattle

2:20 Arrived Denver

3:10 Left Denver

4:20 Arrived Colorado Springs

4:43 Rented Car

5:08 Received phone call from the Bristol house

6/6:30 Woodland Park confrontation

7:20 Received 4 min call from Bristol's phone again (Should have been in Cold Springs.)

8:10 call from disposable phone

8:20 Stopped at Stop N' Go – White pickup

8:36 Shooting

In small letters at the bottom was a list of names.

Mark Archer – insurance money – divorce? Rental car

Joyce Hunter – job security – car

Tiffany Hunter? – a place to live – car

Travis Bristol – hardware store – brown single cab Dodge truck

Glen Hawkins? – hardware store

"You added Travis and Glen to the list but, you didn't mark anyone off yet."

"No, the more I check into this, the more

'people of interest' come out of the woodwork." Hobson took a drink of his cold coffee and set it aside. "Who do we know that drives a white truck? Joyce and Tiffany both drive cars. Travis has a brown truck. What does Glen drive?"

"I think he drives a black SUV. Arnold, Kelly's bouncer, drives a white pickup."

"What would Arnold have to do with Caroline?" The Sheriff frowned at his deputy.

"I don't know. You just asked who had a white pickup." Randy stood and walked to the window and gazed out on the parking lot. "Well, Cynthia who works at the grocery store and Judge Murphy both drive white pickups. I think that other one out there belongs to the Baptist minister."

Both men knew finding the right white pickup was like looking for a needle in a haystack.

Randy sat down and studied the board again, "How do we find out what Caroline was doing from 7:32 to 8:20 without questioning everyone in town? Of course, we are assuming she made it to town by that time."

"Okay, what businesses are open at that time of night here?" the Sheriff mumbled, his mind going up and down the town's major street.

Randy shrugged. "Most businesses close between six and nine. Let's think, after seven: the grocery, drugstore, and hardware stores stay open on Saturdays until nine. Wagon Wheel and the diner would have been open. The gas stations. Stop 'N Go. The motel. The VFW. They were having bingo night. The hospital."

Hobson rubbed his chin. "It's a long shot, Randy, why don't you take the photo of Caroline around and see if anyone remembers seeing her."

"Okay, will do. How about changing the subject? What have you and the DA decided to do about Angie Ehman?"

"Ross won't press charges so the DA just wants to scare her and make her think twice about running away again. I'll talk to Debbie and her husband but we were thinking eight hours in jail when we don't have anyone else locked up and forty hours of community service by July. The DA suggested taking the horse as collateral for the fifteen hundred dollars in county fees that the family owes for the dent in your truck. If Angie doesn't put in the community service, her parents owe another thousand dollar fine."

"I heard Ross' wife already gave her a punishment. She and Van can't hang out with each other for three weeks. Evidently, Van is still upset over her dad being shot. They are hoping that will give Van time to cool off."

"Yeah, Debbie grounded Angie for a month already. I need more coffee." The Sheriff left for the break room and Randy followed.

"Anything I can do to help the investigation?"

Making sure other cases in the office are taken care of, "Did Cary come in to file a report on the missing horse?"

Randy explained, "Yeah, she was in earlier with Joe. Neither of them could figure out how she got out of a locked pasture. Cary said she found the padlock on the ground beside the gate. It is a cheap combination lock. Cary is on her way to buy a better lock. She also found a little horseshoe earring beside the lock. Joe had to pay Dave sixty dollars for the hay the mare ate. Dave mentioned when she found her she had a halter on. No reins or leads were attached. He showed it to Cary; she had never seen it before. She brought it in and I labeled it and put it in storage along with the earring."

"No one had any idea how Joe's horse ended up in Dave Watson's pasture?"

The deputy held out a coffee cup towards the Sheriff who was holding the pot. "No, but they both seem happy now that the horse is back where she belongs and not eating Watson's hay. Did you want me to try getting fingerprints off the halter?"

"No, everything is back to normal. The horse wasn't hurt, right? Only damage was to the hay and Joe took care of that."

"Yeah, everyone is happy."

"Next thing. Any idea when we will

receive the report on the gun and bullets we sent to the state?" The Sheriff handed Randy the cream.

"Well, Dee has connections with one of the lab techs in Denver so she will pick up the report when she goes out on her date tonight."

Hobson slowly shook his head. "The lab tech is one of the several guys on her list of male friends, I assume."

"That very long list, yes. Don't knock it, Sheriff, her list of male 'friends' comes in awful handy some days."

"Does she ever get serious about any of them? Not that I want her to get married or anything." Hobson commented.

"Afraid she'll get married and quit?" Randy smiled thinking of all the sparing the two of them had done over the last few years.

"You're damn right! The worst thing I can think of is her leaving. We would never know what was going on in this office, or the county for that matter. But don't you tell her that. We never want to be in a position where we acknowledge that she runs things. We would be doing our own clerical work, answering our own phones and getting her lunch. We don't want that to happen."

"Sheriff, you are aware that she's taking criminal justice courses online, right?"

"I figured as much. She's smart, competent, tenacious, and she will eat you alive if given the chance. She will make a damn good law enforcement officer."

Hobson grabbed his hat and left.

## CHAPTER 9

Dee entered the office juggling a huge cup of coffee, her purse and a box of donuts. She slid the donuts onto her desk and the two men watched her, both a little somber after Caroline Archer's funeral. "Good Morning, Sheriff. Randy. Can I help you?"

"Right after the donuts, we want the lab report. You remembered to pick up the lab report from your date last night?" The Sheriff reached over to open the donut box.

Caroline Archer's funeral was at the Methodist Church and it was packed with Edna's friends and neighbors who knew Caroline growing up. The minister who baptized Caroline, gave a nice eulogy. They didn't go to the cemetery but were told she would be buried in the plot behind her father. Mark and his sons would stay in Cold Springs for a few more days. Both the Sheriff and his deputy paid their respects to the Bristol and Archer families. None were holding up well. Edna was in a walker with Mary on one side and Sarah on the other. Mark had all he could do to console his sons. Mrs. Bristol's son had not received her message of Caroline's death soon enough to fly back to the States for the funeral.

It made for a reflective start to the day. But, work was waiting.

Rummaging through her huge purse, Dee pulled out a large manila envelope and handed it to the Sheriff. Holding the donut in his teeth, coffee in one hand and the envelope in the other, he headed for his office with Randy trailing.

Getting situated, Clark waited for Hobson to open the envelope. He scanned the report gave it to Randy.

"All of the bullets we sent match the gun?" Randy's eyes were big as he stared at the Sheriff for verification.

"Yeah, it seems like whoever killed Caroline also robbed Kelly. Read the fingerprint report."

Randy stared, turned the page and read. "Travis, Angie and my fingerprints on the Harus. But only Angie's prints are on the handle. An unidentified print on the barrel and another unidentified print on the spent cartridges. Not the same print. Okay, Travis' prints are on the gun-barrel and the cartridges. Well, it's his gun so we would expect that. Angie's prints were on the handle and the barrel, okay. My prints were on the barrel from when I grabbed it from Angie. Those are explained. So, we have two prints we need to identify: one on the barrel and one on the spent cartridges. The same person robbed Kelly and killed Caroline? Maybe?"

"Five people's prints are on that Harus. Randy, call Travis and ask how often he cleans it. And when was the last time he fired it?"

The deputy laid the reports on the desk and went back to his office. The Sheriff stared at the whiteboard and reread the reports.

Ten minutes later Clark returned to the sheriff's private office, "Travis says he cleaned the gun about six weeks ago after he and Arnold shot a half box of shells trying to hit some empty beer bottles. He had a long explanation why it took all that ammo to kill two bottles but I won't bore you with the details. He said they each shot about ten times each. That is the last time he fired it and the last time he cleaned it."

"Thanks for calling him. That doesn't tell us much." The Sheriff got up and took a green marker to the whiteboard and put a check beside the name Travis. Turning to Randy, "We need fingerprints from the rest of these people. I'm sure Mark Archer won't be a problem. I will need a good explanation for Glen though. The Hunter ladies will be a fight if they allow us to fingerprint them at all."

"Kelly will be glad to help us with Tiffany's fingerprints. Oh, I think I've seen Tiffany and her mother in the Wagon Wheel on chicken fried steak night. That's Wednesdays. We could ask Cliff."

"Let's take an early lunch and go do that." The Sheriff grabbed his hat and headed for the door.

Sliding onto the bar stools beside the shiny, old antique cash register, the lawmen nodded their 'hello' to the waitress as Cliff came out of the kitchen with a crate full of clean glasses.

"Morning, gentlemen. And, it is still morning. Early lunch?" Cliff unloaded the glasses behind the bar where the men were sitting.

"Cliff, we've got a favor to ask." The Sheriff surveyed the nearly empty bar making sure no one was close enough to hear.

Moving closer to the Sheriff, Cliff smiled, "Always happy to help law enforcement."

"I'm hungry, can we order lunch first?" Randy had missed too many meals being out on a call. He always ordered first.

They gave Cliff their order. He turned it into the cook and was back to hear their request in less than three minutes.

"Okay, Sheriff, who do you want me to strong arm for you?"

"Nothing so sinister. How often do Tiffany and Joyce Hunter come in?"

"Together?"

"It doesn't make any difference, we need their fingerprints," Randy interjected as the Sheriff drank his iced tea.

"Well, they are mostly here on Wednesday nights for the chicken fried steak. That is the night Margaret takes Edna to the Auxiliary. Tiffany comes in here a few times a week, with Mandy Bristol. You want their fingerprints. That shouldn't be too hard."

Hearing a *ding*, Cliff went to the kitchen to pick up their orders, setting the sandwiches down in front of the officers. "We have a band from the dude ranch coming in to play for the next two nights. I bet Tiffany and Mandy will be in then. I can make sure I'm the one to wait on her. I carry a bar rag with me so I can get her prints without a problem." Finishing his thought process, he nodded, "Yeah, that will work. Anything else I can do for you two?"

Cliff smiled, he was proud of himself for figuring how to efficiently execute the task.

"Sounds like a good plan." Hobson knew he could always count on Cliff Gordon. Cliff served in the Air Force and after his father died came home to run his inheritance -- the family bar and restaurant.

Randy tossed his napkin on his empty plate, pulled out money and laid it on his ticket. "I'll show Caroline's photo around and be back to the office later."

The Sheriff nodded and ordered another iced tea.

* * *


Randy showed Caroline's photo to everyone on the first floor of Mountain View Hospital. Several of the nurses knew Caroline but none of them had seen her on the night she was killed. The deputy got a cup of coffee in the small cafeteria before going to the second floor. He had paid for his drink and turned away. He glanced up and Joyce Hunter was sitting at a table finishing her lunch. Randy stepped out of the coffee line and turned his back so he didn't bring attention to himself but watched her out of the corner of his eyes. She stood, went to the trash and dumped her paper plate and Styrofoam cup in. As she left down the hall, he walked to the trash and peeked in.

He was in luck. There was very little trash in the can and Joyce's cup lay on top. Fishing it out with his napkin, he carefully wrapped the napkin around it and slipped it in his jacket pocket. With a smile, he got his coffee and headed back to the office. He would show Caroline's photo to the nurses on the second floor later. Getting Joyce's fingerprints was an unexpected coup and took precedence.

* * *

Hobson found Glen in his office above the hardware store with the door open. Sticking his head in the room the Sheriff smiled, "Can you give me a few minutes of your time?"

"Sure, Sheriff, come on in." Glen put some papers aside and motioned for his visitor to take a chair in front of his desk.

"I need to ask you some questions about

Caroline Archer and Edna Bristol."

"Okay." He nodded for him to continue.

"When was the last time you saw Caroline?"

"Saw her or talked to her?"

"Both."

"Well, I saw Caroline just after Edna had her knee operation. She was picking up a few things at the grocery store. But, the last time I talked to her was . . . I guess the day before she died. She called me and asked if I intended to take the option and continue the purchase of the store." Glen gestured with his hand to indicate the hardware store. "I told her I hadn't made up my mind. My wife and I have talked several times in the last few months about it. She'sn't too happy with the amount of time it takes away from her and the family. Even though she works here part-time we don't seem to find time for each other. When I worked for Mr. Bristol, I never realized how much work it really took to run this place. He made it seem so easy. Of course, he had run it for years."

Hobson nodded in understanding.

Glen reached over and took out a cigarette and lit it. "Yes, I've gone back to smoking. My wife is not happy with that either. And then there is the money. According to the books and my accountant, I am barely making ends meet. I had to go up on my prices and change some credit terms. That lost me some business. I explained all this to Caroline, and she said when she got back to Cold Springs she wanted to talk to me. That was how things were left."

"Okay, when was the last time you talked to Edna?"

"I'm afraid it was before she was operated on. I've been so busy with the store I haven't even had time to go see her. I feel bad about that. My wife visited her when she was still in the hospital."

"You didn't see or hear from Caroline the day she was killed?"

"No, it was the afternoon before that she called me. She told me she would talk to me the next time she was in town but she didn't mention when that would be." Glen reached over, stubbed out his half-smoked cigarette in the nearby ashtray.

"One other thing. Can I take your fingerprints to eliminate you from the investigation into Caroline's death?" The Sheriff opened the briefcase and took out a fingerprint kit.

His eyes got big with the surprise of the request. Then with a shake of his head and a small laugh, Glen replied, "Sure, why not."

Hobson took his prints, thanked him for his time. Glen tried to clean his hands when the Sheriff left.

* * *

Randy returned to the office and hung up his hat, pulled the cup out of his pocket, and put it in a baggie and labeled it. Giving it to Dee to send to the Colorado crime lab, he explained what it was and how he obtained it.

"Oh." The dispatcher remembered the communication that had come in and handed Randy a Fax from the CBI. The deputy read the report and his mouth fell open. "What?"

Dee turned, "Yeah. When they ran the fingerprints through all the data bases that's what they came up with."

"The fingerprints on the cartridges belong to Arnold DuPree, Kelly's bouncer?" He plopped down in the visitor's chair in the reception area, frowning and thinking.

"Where is the Sheriff?"

Dee looked up from her computer, "Hardware store, talking to Glen Hawkins."

Suddenly he jumped up and grabbed his hat. As he hurried out the door he called to Dee, "I'll be at the lumberyard."

Ten minutes later he searched the lumberyard for Travis Bristol. Seeing his truck parked in back, Randy stepped inside and saw Travis at the repair desk helping an older man unhook the blade off a chainsaw.

When he finished, he walked up to the deputy. "Deputy Clark, how can I help you?"

"Can we talk in the back room?"

"Sure." As they walked by the man at the cash register Travis hollered, "Coffee break." The man acknowledged them.

Sitting at the table in the empty room, Travis asked, "What do you need?"

"Travis, do you remember when we asked you who all knew you owned a handgun? You mentioned Arnold out at Kelly's had borrowed it for a few minutes one night."

"Yeah, I remember." Travis nodded his head.

"Tell me exactly what happened that night."

"Well, it was about two months ago. It was early in the evening. I had just gotten off work and stopped for a drink on the way home. A couple of guys from town had a football pool going at Kelly's and I wanted in on it. I had barely gotten to the door and Arnold was coming out with a young guy in a headlock. I backed up and let them pass. Held the door open for them. I went inside and took a seat at the bar. Arnold came up and asked if I had my gun in the truck. I told him I did. He asked if he could see it for a minute, he wanted to scare the drunken kid he just threw out. I wasn't sure what to do, so I handed him the keys to my truck and told him it was under the driver's seat. He came back in about ten or fifteen minutes later and gave me the keys back. I was kind of uncomfortable with the whole thing. I hurried and drank my beer and snuck out the back door to my truck and made sure the pistol hadn't been fired and was back under the seat. It was there, unfired. Why?"

Randy had listened patiently to the entire story. "Would he have had any reason to take the cartridges out of the gun? His fingerprints were on one of the spent shells we found."

Travis thought. "He might have unloaded the handgun before he used it to threaten the kid. Be sure no one was hurt if the gun went off by accident?"

"Yeah, that's what I'm thinking, too. Thanks for your time. I'll talk to the Sheriff, he may want you to stop by and give us a statement as to what happened that night. I'll let you know. Thanks."

The deputy got up and left.

* * *

Twangs of guitar strings cut through the crowd's conversations as the band tuned up at the Wagon Wheel at 8 o'clock. The bar was full of people. Through the sea of cowboy hats and ball caps, Cliff kept an eye on the door for Tiffany Hunter. The other bartender pulled the taps for draft beer as fast as she could to fill the orders the two waitresses were continually delivering.

Cliff didn't need to wait long for Tiffany to appear with Mandy Bristol. After pouring two soft drinks into immaculately clean glasses, Cliff took the beverages over to the booth where the young ladies sat.

"Can I get you two anything else?" he set the glasses in front of them.

A little bewildered, Mandy glanced at Tiffany, "Yes, I would like a hamburger with everything."

"This is all." Tiffany pointed to the drink. "I've already eaten."

"One hamburger, coming up." Cliff left for the kitchen.

Fifteen minutes later, Cliff delivered the hamburger along with two more glasses of Coke. Sitting in the booth beside Tiffany and Mandy were two young men. One drank beer and the other a soft drink. There were two nearly empty glasses sitting in front of the young man and Tiffany. Cliff hesitated trying to determine which glass was Tiffany's. He set the full glass in front of the girl and knew he had to take a chance. Hoping he was choosing Tiffany's glass, he wiped the corner of the table with a bar cloth and used it to pick up one of the empty glasses by the rim.

Back in the kitchen, Cliff put the glass in a baggie and took it to his office to give it to the Sheriff the next day. His mind kept going back to the two glasses sitting close together on the table. He reassured himself that the one he picked up was Tiffany's.

## CHAPTER 10

The first thing the next morning, Randy showed Caroline's photo around the second floor of the hospital. He left when he spied a neighbor manning the information desk. "Good morning, Mrs. Lambert." Pulling Caroline's photo back out of his jacket pocket, "Did you see Caroline Archer, Edna Bristol's daughter last Saturday?"

Taking the photo and studying it, "Oh, that is a good picture of Caroline. Yes, I saw her that night. She stopped by to ask if Doctor Levine happened to be here. She needed to talk to him. I told her I was sorry, but he spoke to me when he left about half an hour before. The poor woman seemed very tired. I asked her if she had had supper and she mentioned that she hadn't and was hungry. I told her to hurry because the cafeteria closed at eight. I assume that is where she went. I got a phone call and had to take it, so I didn't notice where she went." She handed the photo back to the deputy. "She was such a lovely woman. I just can't understand what happened to her that night. Being shot and all. Those things don't happen here in Cold Springs."

Randy accepted the photo back, "No ma'am, they don't. Thank you for your time and information."

He walked down the hall toward the

cafeteria. He had gotten so excited about getting Joyce's fingerprints the last time he was here that he had forgotten to ask the cafeteria workers if they had seen Caroline. The three cafeteria ladies passed the photo around and one small gray-haired lady came up to him.

"Hello, deputy. Yes, I saw this lady in here a few nights ago." Stopping to think, she added, "She took the last roast beef special we had and a piece of lemon pie."

Clark stuck the photo back in his jacket pocket. "Do you remember what time she left?"

"The exact time? No. I was wiping off tables and Claire still had the cash register open. Maybe about 7:45?"

Pulling his notepad and pen out, "Do you remember if she received a phone call while she was here?"

"Yes, she did. She had ordered, and she stepped over there while I dished up her dinner." The worker signaled to the area by the refrigerated beverages.

"Was she on the phone long?"

"Well, I fixed her plate with the roast beef and cut her a piece of pie. I set them on her tray and moved to the cash register. She reached in and got a bottle of tea and held it up so I charge her for it. Then I probably waited a minute or two for her to finish."

"Thank you. You have been a big help." Randy had a big smile when he left. The investigation into Caroline's lost time was proving fruitful.

* * *

Sheriff Hobson entered the reception area. Seeing the glass on Dee's desk, "Have we collected all the fingerprints we need now?"

Cliff had left the office after giving the baggie with Tiffany's soda glass to Dee. She wrote the pertinent information on it as Randy entered the office.

The dispatch picked up a medium-sized box from the other side of her desk and put the bag with the glass in with the other labeled baggie and the sheet of prints. "We have the fingerprints of Tiffany, Joyce, and Glen ready to send to the State."

"How long will it take to get the results back?"

"Well, if you give me the afternoon off so I can go to Denver shopping, I can drop it off with my friend and see how soon he can finish." With a sheepish grin, she continued, "If I had the whole day off tomorrow, we might have it back by the day after tomorrow?"

Her eyes on the computer in front of her, she silently waited for the Sheriff's response.

The deputy smiled and shook his head as he watched the thought process on Hobson's face.

"Dee, why do you think that everything I ask you to do in this office is negotiable?"

She gazed at her computer screen and didn't answer.

Randy said, "Sheriff?"

With a disgruntled expression, Hobson turned and went to his office. "Shit. Get out of here, Dee! But, I expect that damn state report on my desk first thing in the morning day after tomorrow!" he bellowed.

"Damn, that woman." The Hobson mumbled as he closed the door to his office.

He got aggravated with Dee, one of the most efficient women he had ever met. She was capable of being the office administrator, typist, dispatch, research clerk, and jail matron when needed. She had the mental ability of keeping up with each and every ongoing investigation. Most important, she could get reports and lab results from the State faster than anyone else. She also knew all the law enforcement officers in most of the counties in Colorado and a few in Wyoming and New Mexico. It was one of those situations where it was hard to deal with her but he couldn't run the office without her. The fact she was attractive and added an aesthetic value to the office helped.

Dee logged off her computer, picked up her purse, coat and the box and ran out the door before he could change his mind.

Knocking on the sheriff's door brought Randy a quick, "Come in."

He walked over to the timeline whiteboard and filled in the area around seven o'clock as he explained to the Sheriff what he had learned about Caroline's visit to the hospital the night she died.

"So, we now know what she did for those thirty minutes. There are still holes in the timeline, but things are getting clearer. I talked to Glen Hawkins. He is having problems keeping the hardware store afloat. He talked to Caroline the day before she died. She asked him what he wanted to do about the option. He told her he didn't know yet. She told him they would talk when she was in Cold Spring next time but didn't tell her it would be in the next day or so."

Randy moved the conversation to another point. "You saw the report saying Arnold DuPree's fingerprints were on the spent cartridges? Well, I went to talk to Travis. He felt sure that Arnold emptied the pistol when he borrowed it the night he threatened some young drunk. Travis said he checked the gun afterward, and it hadn't been fired."

"Randy, didn't you tell me Arnold drives a white truck?"

"Yep."

"Time to go talk to him." The Sheriff glanced at his watch, "Do you think he is at Kelly's?"

"Probably."

* * *

When the lawmen got to Kelly's Lounge, they found Arnold's white pickup parked at the side and Arnold was out by the shed moving boxes around.

Randy parked the cruiser, and the men walked over to Arnold. "I can see you're busy."

"Hi, Sheriff, what can I do for you? Did you catch the guy who held up Kelly?" Arnold put the last case of bourbon in the shed and locked the door.

"No, I'm afraid not. We came to talk about something else. Do you have a few minutes?" Hobson walked to the bar's back door, which was propped open with an empty liquor case.

"Sure, do you want to use Kelly's office?" Arnold held the door open for the lawmen.

"That would be fine." Hobson stopped and let Arnold lead the way.

When the men had taken a seat, the Sheriff started, "Can you tell me what you were doing Saturday?"

"You mean Friday, don't you?" Arnold asked thinking this conversation would be about the robbery.

"No. This isn't about the robbery."

"Oh, okay. Saturday. Well, I worked last

Saturday and got here a little earlier than usual. I guess around 5:30. I called Kelly earlier, and he was still having headaches. I worked my shift and left right after 2:00. Why?"

"You didn't go into town earlier that night?" The Sheriff held off telling him what the questions concerned.

Arnold stared at the men for a minute. "Yeah, I went into town. We ran out of Smirnoff and I left the bartender in charge while I went to the liquor store. I was gone about forty-five minutes. Maybe an hour. Why?"

"Did you happen to notice Caroline Archer?"

"Was she at the liquor store? I don't remember anyone there except the owner."

"Do you know Caroline Archer?" Motioning for Randy to give him the photo, "Here is her photo."

Arnold took the photo and studied it for a minute. "I don't know Caroline Archer but I think I saw this lady. When I pulled out of the liquor store parking lot I pulled in behind a car going slow. All of a sudden she swerved into the other lane and came close to hitting another car. She got back into her lane but went even slower then. A few blocks on down, she pulled into the Stop N' Go and I pulled in beside her. The way she was driving I was afraid the woman had been drinking. I wanted to take her home before she caused a wreck. I think it was this woman."

Arnold tapped the photo then gave it back to Randy.

"What happened when you went to talk to her?"

"I went up to the driver's side, and she rolled down the window. I asked her if she was okay. It looked like she had been crying, her eyes were red and she kept pulling tissues out of a box beside her. She said she was fine just wasn't used to driving that rental car. She was upset. Her hands were shaking. I introduced myself and asked her if I could help her. Possibly drive her somewhere. Take her for coffee. Something. She thanked me and said 'no', she would be okay, that she 'wasn't going far'. I said okay and went back to my truck. I waited 'til she pulled out, and I followed her a few blocks 'til she turned off the main street. Was she the woman that was shot?" The Sheriff watched Arnold's face as it dawned on him who the woman may have been.

"Yes. Do you remember exactly when you saw her?"

"A little after eight. I remember looking at the clock in the liquor store thinking Kelly's would be getting busy."

Now it was time for the deputy to ask questions. "Arnold, do you remember borrowing Travis Bristol's handgun?"

He stood a minute frowning, "Okay, look, I know I shouldn't have done it but that damn guy had just turned twenty-one and that was the third night in a row he'd been in there drunk as a skunk. I threw him out twice and he snuck back in while I went after more stock."

"Okay, tell us what happened that night."

"Let me think. The second time he snuck back in, I got him by the collar and took him outside. Travis held the door open for me. I took the guy to his truck, opened his truck door and shoved him in. Like I said, he was three-sheets-to-the-wind. When I pushed him into the seat, he hit the steering wheel with his arm and the horn went off. I was so damn mad at that little shit I wanted to scare him. I remembered Travis had a handgun in his truck. I went inside and asked him if he still had that it and if I could borrow it for a few minutes. Travis didn't want to loan it but I told him I was just trying to scare the guy. After a few minutes, he agreed. When I took the pistol over to the drunk's truck the door was closed and he was leaning back in his seat. I opened the door and shoved it in his face and told him to leave and never come back. Then I slammed the truck door, put the gun back in Travis's truck. Oh, wait, no! Before I went over to the drunk, I made sure the safety was on, took out the shells and put them in my pocket. Then I put the shells back in the handgun before I returned it to Travis. Yeah, that is what happened. Look, that is the only time I've ever threatened anyone with a gun. I swear, Sheriff."

Arnold put his hand up in a swearing position.

Randy reviewed his notes from his discussion with Travis. "Do you remember when all that happened?"

"Oh, let me think. At least two months ago - probably close to three."

"Okay, Arnold, thank you for your time. Clark, are you ready to go?" The Sheriff stood to leave.

When the lawmen got in the car the Sheriff turned to his deputy, "His statement agrees with what Travis told you, doesn't it?"

"Yes. Now what?"

He took a deep breath, "We wait for Dee to bring the fingerprint results back from Denver."

# CHAPTER 11

When Hobson got to his office the next morning, he's secretary/dispatch met him a cup of coffee and a big smile.

"Dee? You're back? Can I assume by that smile you have the fingerprint report already?"

"That would be a very good assumption, Sheriff." Dee handed over a brown manila envelope and waited for her boss to open it.

"So, you are not taking the day off?" He took it and set down his coffee cup.

"Oh, no, I'm taking the day off! My friend starts his vacation today, we're going camping. See you Monday!" Dee grabbed her purse and ran out the door before he got the envelope open.

Randy caught the door as Dee made her exit. "She's back already? Did she get the report?"

Randy silently watched the Sheriff read the paper in his hand. Finally, he burst out, "Well, what does it say? Whose prints are they?"

Looking up and handing the paper to his deputy, "Joyce Hunter."

The deputy stared at the paper.

Motioning for the deputy to follow him, "Let's go to Al's for breakfast and talk this through." Before leaving, Randy picked up the sign to hang on the door. It read *Sheriff's business now being conducted at Al's across the street.*

Seated in their designated back booth, and having given Louise their order, the lawmen sat in silence for several minutes.

The Sheriff absent-mindedly stirred his coffee. "What do you know about Joyce Hunter?"

Clark shook his head, "Nothing much."

"Mary Harris talked to a friend of hers at the hospital over in Gunnison and filled me in on some things. Joyce is a high school drop out, married twice. Her first husband was an alcoholic. Tiffany was by the second husband. She has worked in coffee shops, bars, and cafeterias until she took this job with Edna. Always had a hard time making ends meet. Has a chip on her shoulder. I phoned the police chief in Gunnison. He did a little checking. Other than parking tickets, he only came up with Tiffany trying to sneak into bars and not being of age." Their breakfast arrived, and they ate in silence.

Randy contemplated his empty coffee cup. "I don't know. If Joyce Hunter thought Caroline was coming to fire her, is that reason to kill her? I'm just not getting a good feel why she would shoot Caroline."

"From what Sarah Howard and Doctor Levine told me, Joyce's caretaking of Edna bordered on neglect and mental cruelty. But, that would only result in a misdemeanor charge, with little or no jail time. If of course, we could prove it. When Doctor Levine and Sarah Howard came to explain why Caroline came to town, that constituted notification of possible elder abuse. When I talked to Mary Harris, in her status as head nurse at the hospital, she agreed that with the knowledge we have it would only be neglect and mental cruelty. Should we check for activity along the lines of a felony?" Hobson voiced his thought process.

Randy waved his empty coffee cup at the waitress. "What kind of felony should we be looking for? Fraud? Do you think they are stealing from Edna?"

Having finished his last bite of breakfast and the Sheriff leaned back in his chair, "Let's go talk to Edna before we bring Joyce in for an interview."

Seeing the men stand up to leave, the waitress poured coffee into a to-go cup and handed it to the deputy on his way to the cash register.

* * *

As the lawmen walked through the hospital halls to the rehab area, they could smell the breakfast aromas, but Randy noted the food trays sitting in the halls were well picked over. He felt relieved that they would not be interrupting Edna's breakfast.

Hobson stuck his head around the corner

of Edna's room. "Good mornin'."

"Mornin', Sheriff what can I do for you?" Edna sat in the chair beside her bed with a book in her hand. She pulled her walker in front of her and stood. "Here take my chair. I'll sit on the bed."

The deputy gave her a big smile. "Well, Mrs. Bristol, it is good to see you up and about. You must be feeling better."

"Yes, Randy, I am. These rehab people are a mean bunch, but you can see the results." She stood beside her bed on both legs, holding her hands free and beamed.

The Sheriff took the chair and Clark leaned against the wall. "Do you have some time before your rehab so we can talk?"

Checking her watch, Edna said, "Rehab isn't for two hours. I assume you are here for information. What can I tell you?"

"Has Joyce ever asked for money? Did you ever give her money for any reason?"

"Well, she's always asking for money for this and that. Mostly things like car insurance and gas money, but Caroline gave me strict orders not to give her a cent. If she needed money for anything, she was to ask Caroline."

"Had she ever asked Caroline for money?" The Sheriff shifted in his chair to avoid the sun coming in the window hitting him in the eyes.

"I don't think she ever had the nerve.

Caroline paid her a salary by the month and that included money for food and gas."

"So, you never wrote her a check or gave her cash?"

"No, not to Joyce. I wrote a couple of checks to Tiffany so she could get me cash. I needed to pay the paper boy and George who cuts my grass and cleans my flower beds."

"When did this happen?"

"Right after Tiffany moved in. She's always going somewhere, so I asked her to stop by the hardware store and they would cash my check for cash. Why? Is there a problem?"

"Edna, You are a capable businesswoman but since your operation, have you kept up with your bank accounts?"

"Not like I used to. When you are not able to get around, everything goes to pot. It has been several months since I balanced my checkbook but I checked my bank statements and didn't see anything unusual. Why? You're scaring me, Sheriff."

"Wait! You think Joyce has something to do with shooting Caroline. Don't you? Oh, my god."

Her eyes widened.

Hobson held up a hand. "Take it easy, Edna. We don't know anything of the kind. This is just part of the investigation. Can you call Doug at the bank and ask him to print out all the activity in your account so we can help you go over it? You know, just to make sure everything is okay?"

"Sure, hand me my purse would you? It's in the nightstand."

Randy handed Edna her purse. She picked up the phone and made the arrangements with the bank for the Sheriff to pick up copies of whatever he needed. The men left for the bank.

* * *


Like most small town bankers with a long-term relationship to a local merchant, Doug was efficient and congenial getting the information that Edna needed.

Within the hour, they were back in Edna's room. She had been looking over the statement and the photos of her canceled checks. When she got to the two checks she had written to Tiffany, she showed them to the Sheriff. Then flipping through the rest of the photocopies.

"Wait, I didn't write these to Tiffany. I only wrote her the two checks for $100 each." She continued going through the rest of the canceled checks, then handed the Sheriff three of the sheets. "I didn't write these checks."

He studied the sheets. "This amounts to over twelve hundred dollars. You don't remember anything about these checks? This isn't your signature?"

"I did not write those checks, and that is

not my signature. Look, it doesn't even look like my signature!" The more she studied the checks, the more upset and outraged she became. "Why would she do such a thing? I know she was always asking her mother for money but I don't think she ever got any. Their arguments about money got loud enough for me to hear in my bedroom."

Turning over the photocopies, he noted, "They were all cashed at the hardware store." The Sheriff handed the copies to Randy. "Glen didn't think anything about Tiffany continually coming in with checks to cash?"

"He has several clerks that work there. Tiffany probably made sure a different one cashed them each time." The deputy returned the copies.

"Edna, do you want to file a complaint? Can I keep these?" The Sheriff held up the papers.

"I'm trying to think of a reason Tiffany would do this. I am sure I didn't tell her to do such a thing. No, that is not my signature." Edna couldn't imagine someone living in her own house was stealing from her. She tried to think if she had ever had a conversation with Tiffany or Joyce that could have been interpreted as her giving them permission to access her bank account.

"How about if Randy and I go out and talk to Tiffany? See if there is some reasonable excuse that we can't think of?"

"That sounds okay. I hate to file a complaint if she thought I gave her permission." The pain pills made her mind groggy. She had a habit of sometimes answering questions when she hadn't actually heard what was said. It was not in her nature to jump to conclusions and accuse anyone of something, especially theft.

The men were going out the door. Edna studied the statement again. "Wait, Sheriff! Look!" She held up the statement and pointed to a bank deposit. "Jim, I didn't make this deposit. I don't know what this twelve hundred dollar amount is. It isn't my Social Security or my monthly lease payment from Glen. I don't know what it is. Wait, that is the amount Tiffany took out of my account. Oh, she paid it back." Edna and the two men looked back and forth to one another.

"Yeah, I bet she did," Hobson added the checks up again. "Yes, she took twelve hundred. And, I guess she put it back. Do you have a copy of the deposit slip?"

She flipped through the remaining copies, "Yes, here it is. It just shows 'cash'." She handed it to the Sheriff.

"Can I take this too?"

"Sure, here take the whole thing." Edna handed him the rest of the papers. "Now what? I don't want to press charges. She just borrowed it without my permission."

"We'll go talk to her, see what she has to say and let you know."

When they were out in the hall Hobson muttered, "We found Joyce's fingerprint on the weapon and her daughter writing checks on Edna's account. It's time to talk to the Hunters. I've only talked to Joyce once. She's pretty volatile. I think we need to bring her to the office and question her there. Let her know she can't take control of the interview. What do you think? Bring her daughter in to interview at the same time? They might have done it together?"

"Yeah, I would bring them both in at the same time. See what each of them knows." The deputy agreed.

"Let's drop by the office and pick up your cruiser. I want two cars when we go to Edna's. I don't want them riding in the same car."

* * *

The Sheriff's cruisers pulled up behind one another in front of Edna's house and the law officers went to the door. Joyce's car was the only one in the driveway as Hobson rang the doorbell.

The door flew open and Joyce glared at the men who had the audacity to interrupt her television programs. "What do *you* want?"

"Good morn' Mrs. Hunter. We would like you to get dressed and accompany us to my office. We would like to talk to you about the night Caroline Archer was killed." The Sheriff didn't think her ugly blue housecoat and pink slippers would be acceptable attire if he decided later to arrest her.

"I'm not goin' anywhere with you." Joyce tried to slam the door, but Hobson grabbed it and pushed it inward. Joyce backed up, fled to the living room and plopped down on the couch in front of the TV. The men followed her down the hall and stood in the doorway.

"Randy, why don't you radio Dee, see if she's still in town and tell her we need her help." The deputy nodded as he left for the front yard. Joyce didn't hear the Sheriff. The television game show drowned out all the other sound. Taking the side chair, Hobson folded his arms and watched Joyce.

In the front yard, Randy explained to Dee, that they were at Edna's and Joyce was in her housecoat and wouldn't go to the sheriff's office.

"If she doesn't do what I say, can I knock her around a little?" Dee had taken some self-defense courses last year and was still waiting for a chance to show the Sheriff what she had learned.

"Come on, Dee, get serious. We may need your help."

"Okay, I'll be right there." Dee had been taking courses in criminology at the community college in Gunnison in her off time. She had acted as a matron for female prisoners before and knew the regulations.

Within minutes Dee, now dressed in a long sleeved plaid shirt, jeans, and hiking boots. She pulled up and exited her car. Randy led her inside.

Hobson looked up, nodded to Dee and reached over and used the remote to turn off the television. "Now, Joyce, we would like you to change clothes so we can go to my office and talk. If you need help changing, my deputy, Dee, will help."

"I'm not changing clothes and I'm not going anywhere."

"That is not true. If I need to, I will arrest you and take you to jail just as you are. I can hold you for twenty-four hours without charging you with a crime. If you want a lawyer with you when I interview you, you can call him from my office. Now, would you like to change clothes or go like you are?" The Sheriff stood and Dee moved to stand beside Joyce.

Glaring at Dee, Joyce snarled. "Leave me alone, I can dress myself."

Dee glanced at the Sheriff. "I'll go with you. In case you need help." Dee followed her down the hall to a bedroom and caught the door before it closed on her. She stood inside the door and watched Joyce take clothes to the bathroom and change.

Joyce sat in the back seat of the sheriff's

cruiser and Dee sat in front beside Hobson. Other than the Sheriff asking if Joyce was okay in the back, the drive to the office was silent.

Dee exited the cruiser, waved goodbye and hopped into a pickup with a young man. The Sheriff assumed it was the lab tech from Denver.

Settled in his office with Randy and Joyce, the Sheriff again asked if Joyce wanted a lawyer before he started the tape recorder and they discussed the Saturday that Caroline was killed.

"I don't need a lawyer, I haven't done anything wrong." Joyce's arms were crossed over her chest and her face contorted in a scowl.

Hobson relaxed in his chair, "Let's go over again where you were on Saturday. Start from the morning when you got up."

A heavy sigh was followed by, "I got up and got the old. . . got Edna out of bed and to the bathroom, then back to bed. Fixed her breakfast, gave her the medication. While she was watching the news, I fixed Tiffany and myself breakfast and we ate. I had to go to the grocery store and run some errands. Tiffany stayed with her 'til I got back. Tiffany left then, and I cleaned house and fixed Edna her lunch." She glanced at Hobson. He nodded for her to continue.

"That afternoon, she and I watched a movie. I don't remember what it was. Then we watched the news, and I fixed her dinner. I helped Edna get ready for bed. Watched a couple of programs and went to bed myself. I had just gotten to bed when I heard Tiffany come in. Then, later that night you came and told us Caroline had been shot."

"Okay, you didn't leave the house all day except to run errands in the morning? Is that right?" The Sheriff read from the notes he had been making.

"That's right." She looked down at her hands.

"Tiffany left in the early afternoon and didn't come back until what time?"

"The stupid kid ran out of gas and had to walk home. She didn't get home 'til after ten. Maybe closer to eleven, I don't remember."

"Okay. Joyce, do you own a gun?"

An expression of horror crossed her face. "No. I don't like guns."

"Have you ever shot a gun?"

Joyce looked from the Sheriff to Randy and back. "When I was young, my dad thought I should be able to shoot a gun. He took me out in the country and made me shoot a rifle. The recoil bruised my shoulder, and the sound hurt my ears. I would never shoot a gun again."

"Joyce, we found the handgun that killed Caroline and we found your fingerprints on it. Would you like to explain that?" The Sheriff watched the panic take over her face and body.

She squirmed and her purse fell off her lap and hit the floor. "NO! No, I did not kill

Caroline. Oh, my god. Oh, my god." She gasped. "No. No."

Joyce's breathing became erratic. Her eyes got big and then she started crying.

Randy went to fetch her a glass of water. Upon his return, Joyce's upper body laid across the arm of her chair. Her legs were pulled up to the edge of the chair and she was mumbling through her sobs.

The deputy touched her shoulder and offered her the water and a tissue box. She sat up straight and took slow sips trying to compose herself. Taking a deep breath, "Sheriff I think I need a lawyer. But, I can't afford one." She shook her head, dabbing a tissue at her eyes.

"I'll be right back." The Sheriff left and stepped into Randy's office.

He called the local attorney and asked if he had maxed out his pro bono cases for this year. "Why, Jim? What've you got?" Hobson explained that Joyce was being held for questioning in the murder of Caroline Archer and one of her fingerprints was found on the gun. Clayton agreed to meet with Joyce as soon as he was finished taking a deposition.

The Sheriff went back to his office. "Joyce, Clayton Montgomery will be over in a little while to represent you as a public defender. You can wait in Randy's office or the break room. Where would you like to wait?"

With a resigned sigh, "The break room."

Within the hour a tall man in his forties wearing jeans, a white shirt, and cowboy boots, arrived and introduced himself as Clayton. Immediately he and Joyce were secluded in the deputies' office. "First off, Joyce, do you want me to simply advise you through your interview with the Sheriff or do you want me to represent you if he charges you with a crime? If I just advise you through the interview, then if he files charges, you can ask for a Public Defender. There are some small fees but not near what an attorney would charge. There isn't too much difference for me. Either way, you will get the best advice I can give you."

Looking at the floor, her usual scowl was missing, replaced by pain. "I did not kill Caroline. I don't care if they did find my fingerprint on the gun. I did not kill her."

"Do you want to talk to me about things right now or do you want to talk to the Sheriff?"

"If I talk to you, you can't tell the Sheriff what I said, right?"

"As long as you are not planning some crime spree, everything you tell me will be held in confidence if you accept me as your attorney of record. In other words, tell me you want me to represent you and I can't say a thing."

"I want you to represent me and my

daughter." Joyce watched for his response.

"I'm sorry, I doubt if I will be able to represent both of you, not at the same time. Let me represent you first and then see what I think, okay?"

Her worried expression deepened. "Okay, I guess that will have to do. I know how my fingerprint got on the gun. That Saturday night before Caroline was killed, I heard Tiffany, that's my daughter, come in the house. I got up because she can't remember to lock the doors. When I went to the front door to make sure it was locked, I tripped over her purse. I picked it up, and it felt real heavy. I opened it and found the gun. I don't like guns. I don't know why she had it but I wanted to get rid of it. I got in my car and drove out of town by the river and tossed it over the bridge." Joyce gave a soft sob. She reached for the tissues box on the desk.

"Then you went back to your house?"

"Yes." She wiped her eyes and nose.

"Do you think Tiffany had anything to do with shooting Caroline Archer?"

Shaking her head, "I can't imagine her doing anything like that. I can't imagine her even having a gun. I don't know where she got it. Those things cost a lot of money, don't they? She doesn't have any money. She can't hold a job." She sniffled and wiped her eyes and nose.

"I don't know what kind of gun it was, but they cost a couple hundred dollars, even the cheap ones."

Clayton spoke in his authoritative court voice, "Joyce, my legal advice is this. Tell the Sheriff what you know about the handgun, and how your fingerprint got there. Do you want to think about it for a few minutes?"

"Shit. No, we might as well go tell him." Wiping her eyes again, she stood.

After hearing what Joyce had to say about the gun, the Sheriff had a few questions. "Joyce, when you found the pistol in Tiffany's purse and took it, did you make any stops on the way to the bridge?"

"No. I went straight there. I wanted to get rid of it as fast as I could."

"Do you remember what time you left the house with the handgun?"

"I had been in my room reading. There's nothing decent on television on Saturday nights. It was around eleven, a little after. I was surprised she was home so early. She's generally out until around midnight."

"Joyce, would you ride out with Randy and show him exactly where you tossed the gun."

She agreed. Before they got in the car, "Where do you think I would find Tiffany this time of day?"

With dread, Joyce answered the Sheriff, "She said she was going out to Mandy Bristol's to ride horses." Joyce hesitated before scooting into the passenger seat.

* * *

When the Sheriff got to the Bristol ranch, he saw two riders loping towards the barn. He pulled over to the corral where the young women were dismounting.

Cindy Bristol had seen the sheriff's car drive up and came out the back door and met him at the corral.

"Good morning, Sheriff. I haven't seen you in a while. What can I do for you?"

"Hello, Cindy. Well, I came to talk to Tiffany. Mrs. Hunter mentioned I might find her here." Motioning to the girls who were now unsaddling the horses, he added,

"Yes, you can always find her here. Is she in some kind of trouble? Has she gotten Mandy in trouble?"

"No, only I need to talk to Tiffany." The Sheriff walked to the pasture gate where the girls had let the horses out. Being reassured that the lawman was not here to see Mandy, Cindy walked back to the house and sat on the porch.

"You girls were out riding. I always liked an early morning ride too. Don't have time anymore." The Sheriff's envy was apparent. "Are you getting ready to go back to town, Tiffany?"

She gave Mandy a quick look, "Well, I

guess." It dawned on Tiffany that the Sheriff was here to see her. "Why? Did something happen to Mom?"

"No, your mom is fine. She's waiting for you in my office." Out of the corner of his eye, he saw Mandy edge back to the barn door. "Why don't I follow you back to town?"

It sounded like a request, but Tiffany knew it was not. She swallowed hard, sensing something was about to hit the fan. She wanted to talk to Mandy, but she had disappeared. Tiffany got in her car ready to leave when she caught Mandy peeking out of the barn door. Mrs. Bristol stood on the porch watching.

The pot-holed dirt road leading off the Bristol ranch was slow going for both Tiffany and the Sheriff. He noticed Tiffany's car muffler was about to fall off.

Tiffany used this time to piece together what she thought the Sheriff knew and what she hoped he didn't. The more she thought the more she worried. It was getting bad. When she pulled onto the pavement, she stepped on the gas heading in the opposite direction of town.

Hobson followed her, speeding up enough to keep her in sight. He could see she picked up speed on the flat, straight road. He hoped she knew the road well enough to remember the curve and the steep turns ahead as she went through the foothills. He took his foot off the gas to slow his cruiser. He hoped

Tiffany would notice he was not gaining on her and slow down, too. On this particular mountain road, thirty miles an hour could be dangerous. The two-lane paved road skirted between two mountains going up and down the sides of two more, then leveled into a valley and the road that went to Salida.

Hobson heard the crash of metal hitting wood as he saw the back end of the car go over the side of the road. There was no pull over on his side of the road, so he passed the scene and did a sharp U-turn and found a place on the other side. He hit his blinker and flashing lights. He called for EMS, a wrecker and Randy to meet him at the scene.

Jogging across the road, he realized that Tiffany's car had gone over the embankment rear end first and was wedged between the trunks of two enormous pines. The front tire on the passenger side was still turning. The door was caved in, the result of hitting a smaller pine whose top now lying across the hood of the car. He skidded down the embankment grabbing what scrub oak he could, to keep from falling on his ass and tumbling past the car.

When he got to the driver's side, he had to peek between the branches of the pine to look inside. Tiffany was slumped against the steering wheel and he could see blood running down the side of her head. He tried the door handle and saw the car tip enough that it embedded the bottom few inches of the door into the ground. He tapped on the window to see if he could get Tiffany's attention. She didn't move.

The Sheriff pulled himself back up the hill, grabbing on any root or limb that would help hold his weight. Back at his car, he snatched his flashlight from the dash and the tire tool from under his seat and headed back to the car.

He checked Tiffany again, this time with more light. She hadn't moved. He knocked on the window again. Still no movement. He tried to use the tire tool to pry the door open. Instead, it wiggled the car and dug the door even more into the ground. He didn't want to break out the window but couldn't think of anything else.

Noticing that the back of the car was more stable than the front, he took a swing with the tire tool at the window behind Tiffany. It shattered but didn't fall in. "Dammit," he muttered.

He took a better hold on the tool. It took two more whacks before the window fell in. Thankful the car was still stable, he squeezed as far as could in the window and reached to the back of Tiffany's neck to feel for a pulse.

The touch of his cold hands on the back of her neck brought Tiffany around. She moved her shoulder.

"Tiffany. Tiffany. Tiffany, can you hear me?" He waited for more movement. "Tiffany, wake up! Tiffany!" There was a slight head movement. The Sheriff readjusted his body leaning in the window and tried again for a pulse. She was alive but he could judge better if he could find a pulse.

Jim cursed small two-door cars. He braced his right boot on the trunk of a tree and tried to push himself farther into the car. She turned her head a bit, and he reached for the other side of her neck. She had a pulse, not strong but steady. He reached for the flashlight on his belt. With only his head, shoulder and one arm in the car he couldn't do much but he was able to take a better look at her face and head. There was a laceration on her head and a possible broken nose. He couldn't see anything else.

The Sheriff heard a siren in the distance and climbed up the embankment again. He heard a moan from the car but continued his climb. As he got to the top, he heard his radio chirping static. Someone had been trying to call him. He ran across the road and picked up. Out of breath, he gasped, "I'm here Dee, what do you need?"

"Randy and I have been trying to get hold of you. Both EMS units are busy, one is helping at a wreck on the interstate and the other is on its way transporting a stroke victim to Gunnison. What is the condition of your patient?"

"I can't tell. She's trapped in the car. I can see a head wound and a possible broken nose.

She's unconscious." The Sheriff saw his deputy round the curve followed by the wrecker. "Let me call you back in a few minutes." Randy passed him and drove down to block off the road below.

Within minutes, Randy ran back toting an impressive first aid kit with a manual oxygen pump and a defibrillator. He saw Big Tim's Wrecker Service's Kenworth pulled in behind the sheriff's cruiser. He joined the wrecker driver and the Sheriff who were looking over the bank at the car.

The deputy frowned at the car headed up hill and braced at the back by the two trees. "How did she do that?"

The wrecker driver explained, with her hands in the back pockets of her tight jeans, "I've only seen it once before. She tried to make that curve going too fast, sliding into that tree by the side of the road. She tried to correct. Hit the tree then lost traction in the back, the car swung around and slid down the hill backward. She probably has bald tires and one or more are now flat." She peered over the edge. "Judging by the condition of the passenger side fender, she's likely trapped by the dash and console."

"You are good, Sally. And you are just the one we need right now."

The wrecker driver, a five-foot-two, skinny brunette, pushing forty, looked up at the lawman. "Everyone tells me that, Sheriff."

"Well, in this case, Sally, I need someone to crawl through the back window and see if you can assess the injuries to the driver."

"Do you see EMS stamped on me somewhere? My insurance only covers the wrecking service."

"Okay, Deputy Sally Parker, you are no longer a good Samaritan. You are a member of the sheriff's office. After we use your wrecker to stabilize the car, I want you to crawl in that window and take her vital signs and assess her injuries as best you can." He knew Sally had let her EMS certificate lapse when she went to work for her uncle, the owner of Tim's wrecker service.

Randy, still balancing the first aid kit, skidded down the embankment to the car. Looking inside, through the branches, he could see slight movement and heard a low moan.

He turned to the Sheriff still on the bank and hollered, "We need to lift this tree off the car. Tell Sally to throw me down a cable." While Hobson was bringing down the end of the cable, Randy made his way to the other side of the car to check if the top of the tree was still attached to the bottom. The attachment was only a small fragment of the wood. He helped the Sheriff attach the cable ready for Sally to drag the top of the tree up the embankment and out of the way.

"Tiffany. Tiffany. Can you hear me?" The Sheriff pushed back the pine needles and squinted in the driver's window.

Tiffany slowly lifted her head and turned towards the voice. "What?" She moaned, her eyes slowly opening. "Ohhh."

"You're going to be okay. We're going to help you. Where do you hurt?"

Tiffany didn't answer. Her eyes were trying to focus on the man squinting through the window. She slowly leaned her bloody head back against the steering wheel and closed her eyes.

"Tiffany! Tiffany!" Hobson called out and banged on the window. He could see the blood on her face and the steering wheel, and muttered, "No airbag in that old car, or it didn't go off."

With the tree off the car and the car stabilized with the two cables from the wrecker, Sally and Randy made their way down to the car.

Sally studied the small window behind the driver that she was expected to crawl through and handed the Sheriff the two bottles of water she had brought down the hill. Randy set the first aid kit on the ground and squatted to give Sally a leg up through the window. She wiggled in and slid head first into the back seat careful not to hit the safety glass on the seat. The car quivered and groaned. As she sat up, the car shifted again. She stilled then slowly slid forward on the seat.

The deputy handed her the kit. Sally rummaged through it until she found sterile wipes and laid one on the back of Tiffany's neck. She gently straightened the patient's head and leaned her back against the seat then put the neck brace on Tiffany. With another wipe, she removed the blood from her face. The young girl opened her eyes and tried to focus on the Sheriff who was still standing outside the window.

"Tiffany. Tiffany." Sally said a little above a whisper. "Can you hear me? Do you understand what I am saying?" She cleared away the blood from Tiffany's nose and was working on the gash on her head. There was not enough room for Sally to get into the passenger seat so she worked through the opening between the seats as best she could. Sally slowly lifted her head and turned Tiffany's face toward her. The girl moaned. Sally took it as a positive sign.

"Tiffany, you've been in an accident. You are still in your car and we are trying and get you out. Do you understand?" Sally continued to wash her face. She then reached over and took her right hand and moved it. Tiffany didn't flinch, but when Sally shifted her weight, the car did, too.

Sally hoped the girl didn't notice the car move. "Tiffany, I want you to lift your right arm. Can you do that?" Tiffany moved her hand and arm a few inches.

"That's good, Tiffany. Now move your

left hand."

Her left hand moved to her face. "My head . . . head hurts."

"Yes, I'm sure it does. You hit your head on the steering wheel."

Looking down at Tiffany's legs, Sally could tell that her right leg was pinned down by the edge of the dash.

"Tiffany, does your back hurt? Don't move. Just tell me if it hurts."

"Don't think . . . my head. Who are you?"

"Sally, do you think we can open this door?" The Sheriff's hand was on the door handle. When they attached the cables to the car and with the tree gone, the car tilted back a few more inches. With Randy there the two men could now open the door but he didn't want to try without Sally's assessment first.

The wrecker driver was certain the cables would hold but the movement of the car still made her apprehensive. She knew how deep the ravine was that they were hanging over.

Sally checked the seat belt on Tiffany. It was secure. She checked the neck brace again. "Tiffany, we are going to open the door beside you. If you feel more pain or anything just tell us. Okay?" Sally hoped the car was settled enough with the last little movement that it was secure.

Hobson slowly opened the door. Tiffany tried to turn her head but the brace wouldn't let her. The seat shifted a little and she let out a groan.

Sally leaned into the back seat and motioned Randy closer. "I think her right leg is pinned under the dash. I don't see any blood but I'm sure she can't move it. We need help. This car doesn't have an airbag or at least it didn't go off. I don't want to move her without a backboard."

The Sheriff stood listening.

"I'll call EMS again." Randy took off up the hill.

"My head. . . my head . . ." Tiffany moaned and tried to move.

"Tiffany, Don't try to move." Sally heard a groan come from the car's under carriage. "I don't have much I can give you for your headache but I do have acetaminophen and I'll give you some." She watched Hobson for his approval and he nodded his head. Sally gave Tiffany the pills and a couple sips of water.

When the deputy got back, he assured everyone the EMS was on its way but it would be probably thirty minutes.

Sally made Tiffany as comfortable as possible. Sally was squeezed between the front seats talking and reassuring Tiffany when the injured girl started sobbing. This scared Sally, she thought the pain was worse. "Tiffany, what's the matter? Where does it hurt?"

"I can't mo . . move my leg." Her

shoulders shook as tears streamed down her face.

"I know, it's pinned under the dash. Don't worry, we will get it out as soon as the EMS gets here."

Within minutes Tiffany's sobbing became louder. She kept repeating that it was her fault, and she'd been stupid. The men were leaned up against a tree next to the car waiting for the EMS. They both felt bad hearing the crying and not being able to help.

Sally felt she could give Tiffany one more pain pill, but that was all. She gave it to her, hoping it would help.

Through her sobs, Tiffany gave out a long moan and Sally handed her a wipe and rubbed rub her arm for comfort. Sally sat still, careful not to shift her weight. "It's okay, the medics will be here soon. They can give you something stronger for pain."

"Only my head hurts. I can't move anything else." Sally didn't tell her she was still hooked into her seatbelt, but she didn't want her moving.

"It's my fault," Tiffany murmured. "I shouldn't have taken the money."

Sally didn't understand what she said but decided to silently listen, she figured as young as she was it would probably a family thing.

She sobbed louder. "I shouldn't . . ."

Still patting Tiffany's hand, "Shh, shh, it

will all be okay.

"No." Tiffany glared at the only thing in her range of vision, the steering wheel. She grew agitated. "If I hadn't taken it. I wouldn't be . . . I shouldn't have . . Tiffany tried to unbuckle her seat belt. Sally didn't want to physically restrain her and risk angering her more. If Tiffany had a spinal injury, the last thing she should do was to struggle.

Sally tried to calm her, "It's okay. Your family will forgive you. They will understand."

"Understand?"

"Yes, Your family will understand."

Tiffany quieted down and turned as much as she could to focus at Sally, her eyes big with confusion. "My family? No. . . no. Mom. . . Mom always told . . me I didn't . . have the sense god gave. . a goose. She's right."

After a few seconds the sobbing started again, Tiffany gasped for words, "She's right. She's always right. They'll send me in . . . jail."

"No one will send you to jail. You are going with the EMS to the hospital and they will get you all well. You'll be fine." Sally had no idea where Tiffany's comments were coming from but Tiffany got more and more agitated. Sally wanted to keep her calm and quiet. "You'll be fine. Everything will be alright."

Again Tiffany sobbed, then shouted, "No, they will! They will send me to jail! I took the money! I stole it. You don't understand! It's all my fault." Tiffany stared blankly at the shattered windshield mumbling over and over, "It's my fault."

Sally found a box of tissue in the back seat and set the box on the seat where Tiffany could reach it.

Tiffany's words were running together in a jumble, "My fault. . . fault. . .It's my fault."

Trying to calm her down, Sally set to rubbing her shoulder again, "Shh… Shh… If you took some money, you will just pay it back. That's all. They will understand. Simply work and pay the money back. It will all be okay." She continued to hold her hand.

Sally offered her a drink of water. Tiffany tried to hold the bottle, but it kept slipping through her shaking hands so Sally held it while she drank.

After a few swallows, Tiffany pushed it away. "I paid it back to Edna." She swiped at her nose with her hand, irritated at the trickle of blood. "I had to get the money to pay it back."

"Well, if you paid her back everything should be okay. Now, you just worry about getting well," Sally reassured her.

"No! Now they will send me to jail."

"No, they won't. Why would they send you to jail if you paid the money back?"

Suddenly subdued, Tiffany looked down at her shaking hand with its streak of blood and broken thumbnail. She cried again and mumbled. She swallowed hard, her chest heaving then mumbled loud enough for Sally to hear.

"I . . .robbed . . .Kelly."

"You . . . did . . . what?" Sally was not sure what she heard. She held her hand tighter. Tiffany hiccupped once, breaking her crying fit.

"I had to get money to pay Edna back. Kelly had money. He hated me. He didn't want me around. Him and that bouncer would run me off. He had so much money. I needed it." Her voice broke repeatedly.

Sally strained to listen. Tiffany whispered and her lower lip quivered. She couldn't hear. Sally snuck a peek through the open door to see if the lawmen were listening and if they could hear. They were still leaning against the tree arms crossed, looking at the ground. *Maybe the girl's delirious. She hit her head hard. Is delirium a symptom of a concussion?* Sally couldn't remember but didn't think so.

"How do you feel, does your head still hurt? Are you dizzy? Nauseous? Any ringing in your ears?"

"What? No. Just a little headache and I can't feel my legs." Tiffany tried to turn around and face her, but the seat belt and neck brace allowed only a side-glance. "Oh, god, do you think I'm paralyzed? No! No!"

Her eyes glazed and her breathing was wild. Hysteria was setting in.

"No. Tiffany, no. Please don't move. You can't feel your legs because the blood flow is been cut off by the weight of the dashboard. It's like when your foot goes to sleep. That's all. You aren't paralyzed." Sally hoped that was true. She didn't want to be lying to the girl but she couldn't deal with hysteria.

"Okay, calm down everything will be okay." Sally held Tiffany's hand a little tighter. Then, trying to change to a more pleasant subject, "You were lucky. You didn't go very far over the embankment and those trees caught your small car. You're lucky and you'll be fine. Where were you going? You took that curve pretty fast."

"I ran from the Sheriff." Tears were still falling down her face but the deep sobbing stopped. "It's all my fault."

Silenced by that statement, Sally sat still and held her hand.

"Everything just kept getting worse. I didn't want to talk to her but Mandy insisted. Mandy insisted . . . Mandy was her cousin . . . and she thought she could fix things. No. I should have known better. I shouldn't have gone." A long sigh flowed down with the tears.

Sally didn't understand what Tiffany tried to tell her and she didn't want to know what she was talking about. The sound of a siren broke the silence. EMS was finally there.

# CHAPTER 12

The Sheriff and Joyce Hunter were sitting in the emergency waiting room for the last hour expecting Doctor Levine to come in any minute. When he finally entered, he appeared disheveled as he shuffled over to them.

"Tiffany is a lucky young lady. She has a mild concussion, eight stitches in her forehead and a broken nose. There is a hairline fracture of the fibula bone in her right leg and two broken metatarsal bones in her right foot. She also received a few sprains, strains and bruises. We are putting her in traction. She'll be enjoying a stay in our hospital for a few days for observation. Any questions?" He slid down on the couch across from the Sheriff.

"When can I see her?" Joyce had quit cussing about ten minutes after she arrived at the hospital. She tried to act like a loving mother.

Glancing at the Sheriff, Doctor Levine answered, "She needs rest, and I gave her pain medication. Why don't you wait 'til tomorrow morning?"

"Well, okay, I'll be back then." Joyce walked towards the exit. She needed to talk to Tiffany to find out what kind of trouble she was in. Joyce covered her own ass as far as the Sheriff and the lawyer were concerned. She didn't have any money. At least not any she was willing to give to Tiffany. The girl would be on her own. Joyce squirreled away a little money from what Caroline paid her, knowing that job wouldn't last.

With Joyce out of ear-shot, the Sheriff asked, "When can *I* talk her?"

"I figured you would be interested in talking to Tiffany when I ran into Warren sitting outside the door. He looked like he was getting comfortable with a book and his cell phone. How about early tomorrow morning? The nurses start rousing the patients about six, so between six thirty and seven should be fine."

\* \* \*

By the time the Sheriff got over to Big Tim's, Tiffany's car had been unloaded from the wrecker and sat behind the chain link fence in the yard.

Opening the front door to what used to be a filling station but now held on its shelves the most promising replacement parts for old cars, the Sheriff checked around for Sally.

"Sally, are you here?" Hobson bellowed.

"Yeah, be right there," came a faint answer from somewhere in the back.

Drying her hands on an old towel, Sally stepped around the corner and stopped. "How much of the conversation with Tiffany did you hear?"

"I only caught a few words but Randy heard most of it."

Sally nodded, not volunteering any information yet.

"I need you to tell me what Tiffany said to you."

Sally slid onto the chair behind the old metal desk, "Sit down. I'll try to remember everything."

Hobson moved the yellow tiger cat off the only other chair in the room, sat down and waited.

Sally frowned. "Well, she cried most of the time. In pain . . . her head hurt, so physical pain at first. Then I gave her the acetaminophen, and she felt better. Then she talked about being sent to jail. Something about taking money from a woman named Edna. The only Edna I am acquainted with is Edna Bristol. I guess that was who she meant. She said it a couple of times . . .that she had taken money. Then she said that she had paid it back. I told her if she paid it back everything should be okay. That was when she told me she had robbed Kelly and used that money to pay Edna back. Then, thank heaven, the EMS came."

"Randy said he heard her say something about Mandy talking to someone. Do you remember anything about that?"

"Well, yeah. Give me a second." Sally tried to remember the exact words, "She mumbled something about Mandy wanting to talk to someone and she would fix things. Tiffany kept repeating she shouldn't have done that. Does that make sense? I wanted to stop listening after she admitted to robbing Kelly. Seriously, Sheriff, did that young girl rob Kelly? Wasn't Kelly robbed with a gun?"

"Thanks, Sally, you were a big help, both up on the mountain and here just now. I need you to come into the office and make a statement, Tomorrow or the next day? Also, I need to search Tiffany's car. Is it locked?"

"Yeah, here's the key. I'll try to go by the office tomorrow." She reached behind her taking the key from a wooden board and handed him a tagged key. She walked him out into the yard to Tiffany's car. "Would you lock the car and leave the key in the office when you're through?"

He nodded.

She walked back inside.

He unlocked the passenger's door and opened the glove box. Inside he found the usual papers, a flashlight, lipstick, and gum along with a cute little horseshoe earring. He held it up trying to remember if it matched the earring that Cary had brought in from the stolen horse episode. He pulled a plastic bag out of his jacket and dropped the earring inside. After checking on the floor and under the seats, finding nothing else, he called it a day. He locked the car, returned the key and went back to his office.

                          * * *

Six-thirty the next morning at the
hospital, Warren stood beside his chair and
stretched.  The Sheriff walked up and handed
him a small brown bag containing breakfast
tacos. "Is she awake?"

"Yeah, I don't think she slept well. She
called for a nurse two or three times." Warren
took the bag, opened it sniffed in the aroma.
"Thanks."

"Did anyone try to come to visit her?"

"No."

"Okay. Go home, eat, sleep. If I need you
again, I'll call."

Hobson waved at the desk nurse down
the hall as he knocked on Tiffany's door. He
heard a voice from in the room, pushed the door
open and entered.

"Good Mornin', Tiffany. Can I come in?"

Still waiting for the last pain pill to take
effect, "Yeah."

Tiffany's face was swollen, a small
bandage covered her nose and she had two black
eyes. Her right foot and leg were in a cast being
held up by a traction apparatus.

The Sheriff pulled the chair over beside
her bed and sat down. "We need to talk."

Tiffany turned her face away from the
lawman.

"How do you feel?"

"Terrible. Like I've been in a car accident," she softly commented as she turned to look at him.

"You will be charged you with speeding and reckless driving. But what I really want to talk about is the robbery at Kelly's and the shooting of Caroline Archer."

She closed her eyes and slowly shook her head but didn't answer.

"Tiffany, you may need an attorney. Do you have one?"

Even though she knew this was coming, she was not ready for it so early in the morning. "No."

"Can you afford one?"

"No." She studied her hands and mangled the bed sheets.

"Let me call the judge. He will appoint one for you. I'll be right back." The Sheriff stepped out of the room as he took out his cell phone. The judge referred him to the local attorney like the Sheriff knew he would but he had to go through the proper channels.

"What the hell, Jim, is my number on your speed dial - - BFF or something?" Clayton Montgomery was barely out of bed and not happy to hear from the Sheriff again in two days.

"Now, Clayton, I give you all the business I can." The Sheriff's dry humor didn't cheer up the attorney.

"Yeah, but they're never the paying kind. What do you need now?" With only three attorneys in the county and the public defender seventy miles away, the lawyers rotated pro-bono until charges were filed. And for the next week, everything fell to Clayton until his partners got back from their Alaskan fishing trip.

Jim explained about Tiffany Hunter, the car accident and her conversation with Sally from Big Tim's Wrecker Service.

"Shit. Leave the girl alone. I'll be over to talk to her later this morning. Then we can set up an appointment to meet."

"Thanks. . ." The Sheriff said to himself, hearing the click on the other end of the line.

Hobson told Tiffany that Clayton would work for her pro-bono. The three of them would set up an appointment later to discuss any legal action. He then phoned and alerted the Public Defender's office in Salida. Clayton only advised his clients to protect their rights during the initial interrogation. The Public Defender would be the one representing the client in court.

* * *

Later that morning, Joyce entered Tiffany's hospital room and found the nurse taking Tiffany's vital signs.

"Tiffany, how do you feel? They said you

broke your leg and foot?" Joyce took in her injured daughter. The puffy face, bandaged nose, black eyes, and suspended leg. Noticing the nurse, Joyce rushed to Tiffany's side and patted her hand. "My poor baby." Tiffany was a little beat up but working in various hospitals and delivering patient meals, Joyce saw worse.

Glancing up at her mother, knowing her motherly act was only for the nurse, she sighed, and gave a disgusted, "Hi, Mom."

She didn't want to see Joyce. When the nurse left her mother's attitude would change. Tiffany wasn't ready to be belittled and called stupid. And, most of all, she wasn't ready for the fight that would ensue.

Smiling down at her daughter, "Are they taking care of you? Do you hurt? Of course you hurt, look at you." Joyce was callous to other people's injuries, even those of her daughter. The only injuries Joyce acknowledged were those on her own body.

"Yes, they take care of me. I need pain medication every few hours and they checked on me several times last night." This conversation wasn't going as Tiffany expected. Her mother never did anything without figuring out what was in it for her. Then she realized Joyce was figuring a way to sue the hospital. She remembered all the times Joyce would get angry threaten to sue. Tiffany wondered if this was why her mother came - - looking for a possible lawsuit to get money.

"Are they feeding you? Are you getting enough to eat?"

"Yeah." Tiffany felt the conversation getting weirder; she looked up at the nurse.

"What happened? No one told me. They just told you had been in an accident. Did another car hit you? Did you hit another car?" Joyce got excited.

"No. I ran off the road." Her eyes went to her white-knuckled hands holding onto the top of the sheet.

"Was the road slick? Was there loose gravel? Were you going too fast?"

Swallowing hard, Tiffany glanced at her mother then back at her hands. "I was going too fast."

Here it was. This would start her mother's ridicule.

"You need to slow down. You could have been killed," Joyce said and laid her hand over the daughters. The nurse finished and left the room.

"I was running away from the Sheriff." The words were out of her mouth before she thought.

"What? Tiffany, you had better tell me what in the hell happened!" Joyce's kind voice reverted back to its old ridicule tone.

Just as Tiffany opened her mouth, a man with a briefcase entered her room. "Well, hello,

Mrs. Hunter." He nodded to Joyce. "And you must be Tiffany. Hello, I'm Clayton Montgomery." He offered his hand to the injured girl. "If you agree, I will be your attorney and represent your interests when you meet with Sheriff Hobson."

"Thanks." Tiffany was as glad for the reprieve from her mother and she was glad someone would be with her when she talked to the Sheriff.

Clayton turned to Joyce, "Now Mrs. Hunter, I need a private conversation with my client."

He opened the door and waited for Joyce to gather her purse and leave.

Clayton sat down in the chair vacated by Joyce, opened his briefcase and took out a legal pad attached to a clipboard. "First, Tiffany, you understand about client/attorney privilege and that I cannot tell the Sheriff anything you don't want me to, right?"

"Yeah, I watch all those Law and Order shows."

With a slight laugh, "Okay. Now I am aware basically what Sheriff Hobson wants to talk about but I want you to tell me everything that has happened. We will start with the money missing from and then returned to the personal bank account of Edna Bristol."

With a sigh of relief and a deep breath, Tiffany told her story.

Joyce stood outside the closed door straining to listen, but couldn't hear. She knew it was serious for the attorney to hustle her out of the room so he could talk to Tiffany privately. She waited for a few minutes then saw the deputy returning to his post and left.

* * *

Three o'clock that afternoon, Clayton and Hobson met outside Tiffany's hospital room. "We are waiting for a lawyer from the Public Defender's office. She phoned and said she might be a few minutes late."

Clayton checked his watch.

"No problem." Hobson took a seat in the waiting area. The elevator door opened and a stout, fortyish lady in a black suit and a harrowed expression stepped out.

Dragging her wheeled briefcase and adjusting her shoulder purse, she hurried to the men. "Mr. Montgomery?"

"Yes." Clayton introduced himself and the Sheriff to Sharon Singleton, the Public Defender. Taking a folder out of his briefcase he handed it to Sharon.

"The Sheriff and I will go get coffee while you review my notes. That is your copy. How do you take your coffee?"

With a sigh of relief, she shifted gears from her earlier 'hurry and get there' to the 'I have time to catch up and know what I'm doing'. Smiling, "I like a little cream, thank you."

She tossed her purse on the floor beside her briefcase as the two men left the room.

Ten minutes later the men returned with an extra cup of coffee for Sharon, just as she finished reading the file. She looked at Clayton and gave him an OMG glare. She accepted the coffee, gathered her belongings, and they went to interview Tiffany.

When they were all snugly seated in the small room surrounding Tiffany's bed, introductions made, the tape player turned on, the necessary facts entered into the record Hobson began his questioning. "There is a lot to discuss, Tiffany. Let's start by you telling me about the checks written on Edna Bristol's account made out to you. Edna wrote the first two checks. She remembers writing them. You got her cash to pay the paperboy and the gardener. But she says she did not write the other checks that were made out to you."

He handed copies of the checks to Tiffany and waited for her reply.

Tiffany looked at Sharon and Clayton. They both gave her a nod, for her to answer. "I lost my job and couldn't find one here in Cold Springs. I only wanted enough money to go have a burger and coke once in a while. I needed money, so I wrote those checks. I was only borrowing the money. I was going to pay her back as soon as I found a job."

Earlier Clayton had lectured her on only answering the Sheriff's questions and not volunteering any information. He also advised her on not using the terms: "stealing", "robbing," and/or "shooting".

"You used Edna's checkbook to write checks on her account. Do you remember how many checks you wrote? Do you remember the total amount of money?"

"I wrote seven checks. I think it came to $1,200." She glanced back and forth between the two lawyers. Clayton gave her a slight nod.

"Last Saturday a deposit was made to Edna's account for $1,200.00, that she has no knowledge of. Was that from you?"

"Yes." Tiffany squirmed, "That is when I paid her back."

Sharon interrupted the interview, "Sheriff what are you suggesting Tiffany be charged with?"

"Right now, only speeding and reckless driving." He gestured to her leg hanging from a metal rod in traction.

"Do you plan on charging her with anything else?"

"Let's find out what has happened then we can talk to the DA. Okay, Mrs. Singleton?"

She nodded, looking at the girl's bruised swollen face; she felt sorry for her.

The Sheriff's attention was back to Tiffany. "Are you still unemployed?"

"Yes."

"Where did you get the money to pay Edna back?" he asked.

Tiffany was fidgety but with her leg in a cast, hanging in the air, her movement was limited. She hoped one of the attorneys would say something but they both remained quiet. "I got it from Kelly."

Hobson was used to this kind of slow questioning with a suspect. "Did Kelly give it to you, Tiffany?"

"No."

"Did you take the money from him at gunpoint, Tiffany?"

Putting her head in her hands, she muttered, "Yes."

"Tell me what happened at Kelly's place when you took the money."

Clayton signaled her to tell the story.

"Mandy and I were in Kelly's that evening. He let us in to listen to the band. He served us a Pepsi and only allowed us to stay for the first session then he told us to leave. It was early but Arnold ushered us out the door and told us to go home. I still hadn't found a job. I heard Kelly and Arnold talking earlier that Kelly needed to make a bank deposit that night. I came back before they closed and parked on the side of the building close to the trees. Arnold left and Kelly was over by the shed with the door open. I pulled the hood of my jacket over my head and snuck around the building poked the gun in his back and took the money. Then I shoved him in the shed and left."

"Okay. Where did you find the gun?"

Mrs. Singleton made notes as the Sheriff asked the questions.

"When I got to Kelly's that night it was almost closing time. Travis' truck . . Travis Bristol's truck was still there with a couple of other cars. I thought I would just find something to hit Kelly in the head with and take the money that way, but when I saw Travis' truck, I remembered he kept a handgun under the seat. He never locked the truck, so I got the gun and went back to my car and waited."

"You took the pistol from Travis Bristol's truck?"

"Yes. Travis is Mandy's cousin. Mandy showed me the gun one day when Travis was at the Bristol ranch."

"How much money was in Kelly's bank bag?"

"There were a couple of checks but I tore them up and threw them away. I knew I couldn't cash them. When I counted the money, it was $3,850.25."

"Do you have the rest of the money, after you paid back Edna?"

"Well, I paid Mandy the money I borrowed from her and I bought a pair of cowboy boots. I still have a lot left." Tiffany didn't remember exactly how much was in her purse and how much she had hidden in a book at Edna's. "I'll give the rest of it back."

"I need to know a little more of what happened at Kelly's. When you had the handgun and took the money from Kelly, wasn't there something else that happened?"

Tiffany studied the Sheriff and knew she had to tell about firing the handgun. "Yes, I put the gun in Kelly's back to show him I had a gun. At first, he wouldn't let go of the money, so I turned and fired a bullet into the shed. But it was just to scare him and make him give me the money. I wasn't going to hurt him." She looked at the attorneys who sat quietly and listened.

"Why was it so important to pay Edna back? Could you have simply admitted to her that you wrote checks on her account and agree to pay her back?"

"No. I knew from the phone conversations Edna had with her daughter that things weren't going well for Mom. I could never admit I had written those checks. Mom kept saying I needed to stay on the good side of Edna or Mom would lose her job and we wouldn't have a place to live."

Tiffany paused, working up the nerve, "I like living in Cold Springs, I like riding horses with Mandy and I like listening to music at Kelly's and the Wagon Wheel. I've never had a friend like Mandy before. I just wish I could find a job."

"Could you have borrowed the money from your mother to pay Edna back?" Sharon tried to understand why Tiffany thought robbing Kelly's was the only option.

The girl shook her head and looked at Sharon like she was crazy to even bring up the subject. "Tell my mother that I had written those checks and ask her for a loan to pay it back? No, she wouldn't give me the money. She would throw me out of the house!"

"Okay. Do you remember anything about the Saturday after that . . . the evening Caroline Archer was shot?"

Tiffany glared from one attorney to the other, "Aren't you two supposed to tell me not to answer these questions?"

Clayton answered, "Tiffany, the Sheriff already knows everything you have told him so far."

"How does he know?" Alarm crossed her face.

"Tiffany, I investigate. I talk to people and find out things. I talked to Edna, she told me about her bank account. I am aware the handgun belongs to Travis Bristol. I know that you were in possession of the gun on the night Caroline died." The Sheriff didn't want to say too much, but he did want to let her think he knew more than he did.

She took a deep breath for courage. "I

knew Caroline was coming to see Edna. I heard them on the phone. I knew Caroline would find out about the checks so I wanted to tell her first and let her know that I had paid the money back."

Tiffany kept looking at the attorneys for advice. Clayton was stone-faced but Sharon looked apprehensive. Tiffany realized she wasn't getting any type of reprieve so she continued. "I called and asked to talk to her. She said she was at the hospital and I could talk to her there. Mandy and I went there and saw her as she was coming out. I explained everything, and she just got really mad. She threatened that she would tell the Sheriff and she would make sure Edna pressed charges. Mandy and I both pleaded with her but she wouldn't listen. She said she would throw Mom and me out the minute she got to the house."

Tears came to Tiffany's eyes, "She left the hospital. Mandy and I talked about what to do then we left too. We saw her later pulling out of the Stop N' Go and followed her. I honked, and she pulled over at that bed and breakfast place. I parked by the street and Mandy and I got out and walked up. Caroline opened the car door. She was still real mad. She said she was tired of listening to us and started to get back in the car. I pulled the gun out of my purse. I only wanted her to stop and listen to us. Then I heard a noise behind us." She reached for a tissue and blew her nose.

"I turned to look over my shoulder. It was Arnold from Kelly's. He was walking towards us. He asked, 'What's going on, Ladies?' Then he saw the gun and reached his hand out for it. He said, 'give me the gun.' You know, in that deep stern manner he has. I handed it to him. Caroline was hollering something about us being thieves and we should be in jail. Arnold turned to Mandy and me and told us to leave and meet him in front of the Wagon Wheel. Mandy and I both turned and ran."

By this time tears were streaming down Tiffany's cheeks and she was wiping them away with tissues.

"What happened then? Did you go to your car?"

Nodding her head, "Yes, we got in the car and went straight to the Wagon Wheel like he told us to. We sat out front and waited for him. It wasn't long before he got there. He told us to go home and not say anything." She looked up, shame in her eyes, "I asked him if he would give me the handgun so I could give it back to Travis. He hesitated, but I convinced him I wanted to return it. Arnold finally gave it back. I was going to return it but I couldn't find it the next morning."

"Tiffany, did you hear a shot when you went back to the car?"

"No. I don't think so. I don't remember.

All I know is I was really surprised when I heard Caroline had been shot."

Sharon looked at the Sheriff, "Did this Arnold call 911?"

"No." The Sheriff shook his head, "It was called in by the owner of the B&B."

"What happened after you left the Wagon Wheel?" Hobson was eager to be gaining new facts.

"Well, I took Mandy home. But, I ran out of gas and borrowed a horse. Mandy had left a halter and a new set of reins in my car. I used them to ride a horse back home. I put him in a pasture right outside of town and walked the rest of the way to Edna's."

Everyone in the room sat still, playing over the conversation, thinking.

Tiffany was mumbling to herself. The Sheriff leaned in, hearing her say over and over. "I just wanted her to stop and listen. That is all. I just wanted her to listen."

"Sheriff, do you have any more questions?" Clayton stood and pushed his chair back.

"No, not right now." He turned off the tape recorder and put it back in the case.

Tiffany pleaded, "Sheriff, I can give Kelly most of the money back. I still have it at the house."

The Public Defender stood, and put Tiffany's comment in legal terms, "She has agreed to make restitution here, Sheriff. No one was hurt."

He acknowledged this with a nod.

Sharon stepped closer to the bed and Tiffany told her where she had put the money. The Defender nodded her head and assured her that she would turn the money over to the DA.

In the hall outside Tiffany's room, Sharon stopped the Sheriff, "What are you going to ask the DA to charge her with?"

"Ma'am, right now I need to go find and arrest a very large bouncer. I'll let you know after I do that and talk to the DA." Taking out his cell phone, he spoke into it, "Randy, I'm coming by to pick you up. We're going to arrest Arnold DuPree for the murder of Caroline Archer."

\* \* \*

There were several cars in the parking lot and Kelly was standing in the doorway of his bar when the sheriff's cruiser drove up. The lawmen got out of their car.

"Kelly, is Arnold around?" The Sheriff stern expression made Kelly step back so they could enter the bar.

"No, he's not, Sheriff. But he left me the two hundred dollars he owed me and he left you a letter." Kelly went behind the bar, reached under it and pulled out a legal envelope with

'Sheriff Hobson' written across it.

Taking the envelope, the Sheriff tore it open and read. Halfway through, he decided, "I might as well read this out loud."

'Sheriff,

I want you to know that Mandy Bristol and Tiffany Hunter had nothing to do with the death of that lady, Caroline. (I don't remember her last name.) I took the gun from the girls and told them to leave. When I did that, this woman got even angrier. I tried to calm her down, but she was so upset she wasn't thinking straight. She grabbed the gun, and it went off. I'm sorry it happened, but it was an accident.

Tell Kelly I appreciate everything he did for me, but I need to move on now.

Remember the girls had nothing to do with the accident.

Arnold DuPree.'

"I'm going to assume that Arnold has left the county." The Sheriff looked at Kelly.

"I would imagine he has left the state. No, I have no idea where he would have gone. He hasn't been to work in the last two days. I'm not sure that is even his real name. He left his truck with the title and told me to sell it and give the money to the Methodist Church."

"You couldn't have brought me this

envelope sooner, Kelly?" He gave the bar keeper a pointed stare.

"Sorry, Sheriff. I wasn't aware it was urgent."

Randy sat down on the barstool. "How did he leave town? Did he own another car?"

"No idea. When he first came in here about six years ago, he was riding an old Harley that sounded about to fall apart. He had a couple of beers and asked if I knew of anyone that needed help. I asked him what he could do, and he rattled off everything from house painting to being a bouncer and I stopped him right there and gave him a job. He helped me with everything around here from plumbing to bouncing. I really hate to lose him but I always felt that he might pick up and leave at any time."

"He had an apartment over across from the high school, right?" The Sheriff got up to leave.

"Yeah. Number two. I drove by there this morning and knocked on the door. No one answered."

"You know of anyone he was close friends with?" the Sheriff knew there was no hurry to get back to town, so he sat back down.

"Me. If people didn't give him trouble, he was nice to them. But, I'm not aware of any close friends here in Cold Springs. He was always protective of the women that came in here, but I don't think he ever dated any of them. I knew very little about him. I think he traveled a lot before he got here. He didn't have a girlfriend that I know of. He never got any mail here. I don't think he had a bank account or any credit cards. I always cashed his paychecks for him."

"Did he have any run-ins with the law before he came here?" The Sheriff motioned to the coffee pot on the counter behind Kelly.

Setting cups of coffee in front of the lawmen, Kelly said, "He never talked about any problems. Oh, there was a woman that come by about a year ago looking for him. I gave her his address, and that was the last I saw of her. I asked him if she had found him and he said she had. Didn't give me any more information than that. I got the impression he wasn't too happy to see her."

"I'll put out a bulletin on Arnold as a person of interest in this investigation." He drank his coffee, paid and got up to leave. "You'll let me know if you hear from him, right? And do it in a timely fashion?"

"Of course," Kelly put the dirty cups in the tub behind the counter.

* * *

The lawmen were back in the office after checking Arnold's apartment. His manager said Arnold had moved out of his one-bedroom apartment night before last, leaving the furniture. He left a note saying that the next renter could have it if they wanted. He did not leave a forwarding address nor did he ask for his deposit back.

The lawmen were in the sheriff's office discussing the best way to find the missing bouncer since they had little and nothing to go on. As far as they knew, Arnold was on foot. The closest car rental place was forty miles away. They had put out a 'person of interest' bulletin. The Highway Patrol was on the alert for a hitchhiker of his description. They were busy brain-storming.

Suddenly they heard Dee's loud voice by the front door. "Hello, Arnold, what can I do for you?"

Both men gave each other a surprised look, jumped out of their chairs almost hit each other going through the doorway and ran to the front. They come to a halt at the reception desk. "Arnold." Jim looked at the bulky disheveled man carrying a duffle bag.

"Sheriff. I bet you want to talk to me."

"Oh, yes!"

Arnold put the bag down beside Dee's desk and the Sheriff led the other two men back to his private office. They sat down and the Sheriff placed a tape recorder in the middle of his desk. Arnold nodded his head towards it.

"We were under the impression that you had left town." He turned on the recorder.

"I did. I came back. I like Cold Springs. I like working at Kelly's."

"Okay, would you like to tell us what happened when Caroline Archer died? And, why you left town." He started the recorder.

Arnold answered the shorter question first. "Sure. I left town because I probably have a warrant out for my arrest in Arkansas. I got into a brawl down there and a couple of guys got beat up pretty bad. There was also a problem in Missoula, Montana. I don't know what the status is on either of them. They both happened several years ago." He looked around. "Can I get some coffee?"

The Sheriff nodded and Randy left to fetch the coffee.

With their thirsts satisfied, Arnold began his story. "I told you about seeing this car driving erratically and how I stopped at the Stop 'N Go to see if the woman was okay. Remember?" The Sheriff nodded.

"Well, I followed her for a few blocks like I said. I was a block behind her when I saw Tiffany's car honk at her and she pulled into that bed and breakfast. I watched a few minutes Tiffany and Mandy seemed to be arguing with the lady and I decided I needed to find out what was going on. I was afraid those two kids were about to get in trouble and the woman driving the car wasn't in good shape either."

He hesitated and looked at the Sheriff

then continued. "As I got close, Tiffany pulled a handgun out of her purse. I walked up, asked her for it and she gave it to me. I checked that the safety was on and told the girls to leave. I told them to meet me in front of the Wagon Wheel. They left, and the woman got even more upset because I had gotten involved and told the girls to leave.

Arnold sighed and repositioned himself in the chair. "She threatened to call the law on the girls and me. The woman was getting irrational. She was so agitated there was nothing I could do or say to calm her down. I told her I would call the Sheriff for her. She needed help. I put the gun in my left hand and started to take my cell phone out of my pocket. She reached for the handgun and it went off. I swear, Sheriff, the safety was on. I don't know what happened."

Arnold continued, "Anyway, I tried to check for a pulse. I couldn't find one, but half the time I can't find my own pulse when I'm working out. I pulled off my shirt to try to stop the bleeding then I heard a car coming. I panicked, just like I always do. All I could see was a jail cell ahead of me. I ran back to my truck and left for the Wagon Wheel. When I got there, the girls were waiting. I told them not to talk about their fight with the woman and Tiffany wanted the gun back. It belonged to Travis Bristol, and she wanted to return it. I was stupid, but she begged and started to cry so I gave it back to her."

Arnold finished the last of his coffee and waited for the Sheriff to say something. "It wasn't a smart move. I should have stayed and called 911. I hung out with a rough bunch down in New Orleans when I was young and my instinct is always to run."

Hobson turned off the recorder. He pointed to the driving glove on Arnold's right hand. "What's with the glove on the hand?"

"It's easier to hide it than to explain." Arnold took off his glove and revealed an impressive scar running from his little finger across the back of his hand to his wrist. Two of his knuckles were bulkier than the others and disfigured. Then he turned his hand over and there was a mangled scar in the middle. "I did a lot of bare knuckle boxing when I was young. It doesn't affect movement but the nerve damage is extensive. My hand is painful and stiff if it gets cold. The glove helps keep it warm."

The Sheriff understood. "Arnold, I'm going to lock you up for a few hours. I need to check on several things. Do you mind following Randy back to the cells?"

"Have you fed lunch yet? I didn't have breakfast," Arnold stood to go with Randy.

"We can order you something from the Wagon Wheel," the deputy assured him.

Randy locked Arnold up in a cell while Dee went to order his lunch. Standing by the door to the sheriff's private office, "Hey, Jim, who gets to talk to Mandy?"

"Go out to the ranch and talk to her. See if she says anything different from Tiffany and Arnold. I'll check on outstanding warrants for Arnold."

* * *

Hobson had made the rounds of the county judge, the district attorney, and Edna. He was opening the courthouse door when he saw Mandy Bristol and her mother leave.

Entering the office he saw Randy, "What did Mandy say?"

"Told the same story as Tiffany and Arnold. Didn't add anything but a lot of crying. Her mom was fit to be tied. That girl won't be able to leave the house 'til she's thirty."

"I wish all the high school kids would stay locked in their rooms 'til they are thirty." The Sheriff always indulged in wishful thinking.

"What about Arnold?" Randy followed the Sheriff back to his office and sagged down in the chair.

"I checked and the only outstanding warrant is old and no longer in effect so he is clear there. I talked to the DA. He wants you, me and all the evidence in his office at ten tomorrow. I also talked to the judge he would like everything settled as quickly as possible. We can schedule a hearing or an inquest for sometime next week if we are sure we have everything we need. We will find out how close we are to a hearing when we talk to the DA tomorrow. Anything you can think of we need to do or anyone we haven't gotten statements from?" The Sheriff's haggard look reflected the time, energy and worry that had been put into investigating this death.

# CHAPTER 13

The next morning at ten o'clock the three were all vying for a place to sit in the conference room of the District Attorney's office. The DA sat at the head of the small table; to his right were Sheriff Hobson and Randy Clark. Spread out across the table, were all the written statements the law officers had gathered during the investigation.

The DA was a short, slender man in his fifties with salt and pepper hair, unruly eyebrows and a small mouth. He was chomping on a piece of gun. He had decided Monday to quit smoking again. Leaning back in his chair with his arms across his chest, he said, "Tell me what's been happening, Jim."

"Okay, I'll try to make this as brief and uncomplicated as possible." The Sheriff picked up the first set of papers.

"First, we have Tiffany Hunter's statement admitting she had been writing checks on Edna Bristol's checking account without her permission. The total amount that was taken was $1200.00."

"How old is Tiffany? Is Edna going to press charges?" The DA picked up a pen and took notes on a legal pad.

"Tiffany is nineteen and Edna probably won't press charges. She thinks Tiffany is in enough trouble. And, she did pay it back."

There was a head nod from the DA.

"Next, Tiffany admits that she took Travis Bristol's handgun from underneath the front seat of his truck that was parked outside Kelly's Lounge. She waited several hours until Kelly closed the bar and then proceeded to use the gun to rob Kelly of five days receipts in the amount of $3,910.90. That is the entire amount including checks. Kelly resisted handing over the bank bag and she shot the gun, putting a hole in the shed. Kelly let go of the bag and she hit Kelly on the side of the head and pushed him into the shed and locked it. Arnold DuPree, Kelly's bouncer, found him a little while later and let him out. He had a bump on his head was all. He is fine now."

The DA sighed. "We have Tiffany for the gun theft and armed robbery, right?" He was taking notes as fast as he could.

"Yes, she admitted to both in a statement in front of her attorney and a Public Defender." He set that pile of papers by the DA and picked up the next batch.

"Now, the death of Caroline Archer. According to the affidavits of Tiffany Hunter, Mandy Bristol. and Arnold DuPree: Mandy and Tiffany talked to Caroline at the hospital and told her about taking Edna's money and then paying it back. Caroline wasn't happy about it and threatened to press charges against Tiffany. And, she threatened to throw Tiffany and her mother out of Edna's house where they were living. Later, after they all left the hospital, Tiffany honked and stopped Caroline again in the parking lot of the bed and breakfast. At that time Mandy and Tiffany got out of their car and went to Caroline's car."

Hobson was reading from a document and paused to make sure the attorney was still following. "They were arguing when Arnold went up to them. He saw that Tiffany had a gun in her hand. He took it from her and told the girls to leave and go to the Wagon Wheel. Caroline became enraged that he interfered with the confrontation and grabbed for the gun. The gun went off and Caroline was shot. Arnold said he checked for a pulse but couldn't find one. He panicked. He has a police record for fighting. He left the scene instead of calling for help."

He paused again and looked at the DA. "Actually, I think he left town or at least intended to but he came into my office yesterday because he wanted to make sure that the girls didn't get in trouble for the shooting. He is now sitting in one of my jail cells."

"All of these statements agree that's what happened?"

Both lawmen nodded their heads 'yes'.

"Okay. Have you talked to Doctor Levine about an inquest on the death?" The DA flipped over the page on his legal pad.

The Sheriff pushed more paper over to

the DA "He asked about it, I told him I would check with you."

"It sounds like we need one, just to make sure. I'll call him and make arrangements. I want to attend."

"Next it seems that Tiffany took Mandy home and on the way back into town, she ran out of gas. At which time she borrowed Joe McCall's horse and rode it as far as Dave Watson's place before she left it in his pasture."

Dropping his elbow to his desk and putting his head in his hands, the DA muttered, "Horse theft? You're kidding me?"

The Sheriff shook his head, "Afraid not."

The DA looked up with a snarl, "Am I supposed to prosecute her for horse theft, too?"

With a slight chuckle, Hobson gave an assurance. "No. The horse is none the worse for wear. Joe wants to be reimbursed for the feed bill Dave charged him."

"Good." He started to pick up the papers the Sheriff had given him. "How much was the bill?"

"Sixty dollars." He smirked.

"That must have been damn good hay!" The DA shook his head.

"Okay, next thing, the gun." Randy handed the Sheriff the next pile of papers.

"There's more?" the DA scowled and gave a long exhale.

"Yes, after Caroline was shot, Arnold

gave the handgun back to Tiffany.

"Why? Why! Why would he return the gun to this crazy young woman?"

The Sheriff hated to try to explain Arnold's logic. "She wanted to return the gun to its owner."

The DA gave a chuckle and then shook his head. "The girl committed armed robbery but wanted to return the stolen gun to her friend. Okay, go on. This saga has an end doesn't it?" He leaned back in his chair ready for the next segment.

The Sheriff looked down at the paper without answering, "Tiffany took the gun home in her purse. Joyce, Tiffany's mother, found the gun and took it and threw it away down by the river."

"And?" He knew there had to be more. There were too many piles of paper still on the table in front of the Sheriff.

"And, that is when our runaway, Angie Hudson found the gun."

"Hold it, she's the one who shot Ross Campbell, right?" The DA was trying to follow all the legal ramifications of what had happened.

"Right."

"Sheriff, do you have that damn gun?"

"Yes, I do. Oh, I want to show you an article from last month's Denver Post."

The DA read the paper he was handed.

When he had finished, "You're telling me

that this handgun that has been causing all the problems in Cimarron County is a Harus? The same kind of gun that the Federal Government talks about in this lawsuit against the foreign manufacturer? The gun the government is forcing this company to recall because of a defective safety and firing mechanism? This Harus gun that has all of these instances of firing on its own, " he pointed to the article, ". . is the one that caused the death of Caroline Archer?"

"Yeah. And, also caused Ross Campbell's injury." The Sheriff knew that evidence alone would either rule Caroline's death an accident during the inquest or be the legal defense for Arnold DuPree.

The DA looked angry enough to set fire to the paper on his desk. Almost turning red in the face trying to hold back his fury, he firmly stated, "Find out if we have any more guns in this county that needs to be returned to the manufacturer. Put an ad in the county paper and bill my office." Then under his breath, he murmured, "and the damn laws says we can't hold gun manufacturers liable."

With another deep breath, the DA swallowed his anger and continued, "Okay, back to the original discussion. The problem with Angie Hudson has been taken care of right? She's in parental custody. She got a day in jail and community service plus a fine she has to work off. Oh, yes, and her horse was confiscated.

I remember. I'm glad Susie Wheeler had room at her rescue ranch so the county won't be paying for feed."

The Sheriff nodded his head. "Yes, that's right. Susie is a great asset to this county. Angie Hudson has a lot of growing up to do but I think that is beginning to happen now."

"What else? I have a feeling this isn't the end of the story."

"No, not quite."

"The saga continues," the attorney mumbled.

"When I went out to the Bristol ranch to talk to Tiffany, she took off in her car and ended up missing a curve. She has a broken leg and foot. She's in the hospital in traction."

"I assume I add reckless driving to the list of charges against Miss Hunter?" The DA leaned back in his chair with his fingers held in a peak over his chest. "You have this infamous handgun in your possession and the young woman is in the hospital in traction. Do you think the Cimarron County crime wave is over for awhile?"

The Sheriff and the DA both shook their heads and spent a few minutes contemplating how the people's continuous bad decisions combined with a faulty gun had led to the past events in Cold Springs. Then their minds came back to the present.

The District Attorney had made his

decision. "Tiffany is still in the hospital?" The Sheriff nodded. "When the doctor releases her, arrest Tiffany for the theft of the handgun and armed robbery and reckless driving."

"Okay. That won't be for a while." The Sheriff stood to leave.

"I will contact Doctor Levine to set up the inquest for Caroline Archer. After that, I'll talk to the Public Defender and see if we can work something out for Tiffany Hunter. I'll let you know about the inquest." The DA stood to show the men out.

# CHAPTER 14

Three days later, Randy, Dee and the Sheriff were back in the office after the inquest into Caroline's death. The coroner's panel had heard from Kelly, Edna Bristol, and Mark Archer, that to their knowledge Arnold DuPree and Caroline Archer had never met before. They then heard Arnold tell the detailed account of the encounter between Caroline and him. The letter from Arnold addressed to the Hobson was also introduced but Arnold and the Sheriff explained it to the satisfaction of the panel and the coroner.

However, it was the manufacturer's recall of the gun for safety reasons that sealed the decision. The three women and three men inquest panel decided that the death of Caroline Archer was an unfortunate accident.

Randy mentioned that while the Sheriff was talking to the DA, Doctor Levine told him that Tiffany would be released in two days. There were four jail cells behind the sheriff's office in the courthouse basement. The first cell had been petitioned off to allow a woman prisoner more privacy. That would be where they would hold Tiffany after her arrest. Dee would act as a matron for the jail like she always did for female prisoners.

*  *  *

Sunday morning a criminal complaint was officially filed, Tiffany was arrested in the hospital and taken to the Cimarron County jail. Monday would be her first court appearance in front of the county judge.

Doctor Levine insisted that Tiffany needed a wheelchair at her disposal because her leg still needed to be elevated. Randy wheeled her into the sheriff's office. The swelling in her face had gone down but around her eyes, it was still blue-green. She had a cast from above her knee down to her foot with only her big toe showing. Her fingerprints and photograph were taken, and she called the phone number the Public Defender had given her the last time they met.

"Would you like to call your mother and tell her where you are?" Dee offered after she had talked to the Public Defender.

Tiffany hadn't heard from her mother since she was first taken to the hospital. "No, thank you." Tiffany put her head down ashamed that the people in Cold Springs knew what kind of mother Joyce was. It hurt Tiffany again having it reinforced that her mother didn't care about her.

Tiffany was taken back to a cell that had been furnished with a small recliner and nightstand to accommodate her broken leg. The small cell was a bit cramped with the extra furniture, the cot and the stainless steel sink and toilet. Mandy and her mother had stopped by earlier to drop off several horse magazines and a comforter they thought Tiffany might enjoy.

Randy was wheeling her into the cell when Tiffany put up her hand so he would stop. She put her face in her hands and sobbed. The deputy called for Dee to help; he didn't like dealing with emotional women. Dee signaled for him to leave and went over to the young girl, rubbed her shoulders and offered her a box of tissues. She waited until Tiffany had composed herself then pushed her into the cell and stopped the wheelchair beside the bed.

"Would you like me to help you onto the chair or the bed? I need to keep the wheelchair in the office."

"The chair, please." Dee helped her into the chair and reclined it back so her leg us elevated.

"Mom always told me I would end up in jail. I've made a mess of my life." Her voice caught on a sob.

Dee sat on the cot. "Most people who end up here have. All I can suggest is to cooperate with everyone who is trying to help you and make good use of your time here." The office assistant didn't know how long that would be.

Dee went to the sink, got her a glass of water and handed it to Tiffany. She gave Dee a half smile to show her appreciation.

"Did you graduate high school?"

Again the tight-lipped half smile, Tiffany said, "No, I quit my junior year but the school counselor helped me pass my GED. She was real nice. She lived down the street from us. She helped me a lot. Mom didn't care if I went to school. She wanted me to quit when I turned sixteen and go to work full time."

"It's great that you got your GED. Better than a lot of people."

Tiffany looked up at Dee again. "Did you finish high school?"

"Oh, yes. My parents would have been very unhappy if I hadn't."

"My mom didn't care if I graduated or not, just so I went to work full time and help pay for rent and food. I worked part-time my sophomore and junior years in high school at a diner in Gunnison. After I quit school, I went to work full time until I got fired. They said I flirted too much with the men. But, if you flirt and are nice to them, you get better tips. I would only give my mom my paycheck and half of the tips. I kept the rest. If she had known I had money, she would make me give it to her."

"I'm sure that's true. Did you want to go to college or beauty school or something?"

Tiffany had quit crying and seemed to feel better.

"I didn't want to go to college, but I

wanted to work in an office. I guess that will never happen. I'm stupid and ugly." The sniffling started again.

Dee changed the subject, "What has your attorney told you?"

"Not much of anything. They haven't told me what I will be charged with but she said I could get over ten years in jail with all the charges." Her shoulders sank and she looked at her leg, held up by the recliner. "The doctor said I might have a slight limp, too." The crying started again with a wail. Tiffany's hand was full of tear-stained tissues and Dee set the small plastic wastebasket by the chair.

"Tiffany, the doctor gave us your pain medication. You are due for a dose in twenty minutes. Do you want it now?"

She nodded her head and Dee went to get the meds. Randy was coming out of the break room and met Dee.

Randy softly asked, "How is she doing?"

"This wasn't how she expected to spend the next few years of her life. Have you seen her mother around anywhere?"

He thought a minute. "No, I don't think so. Did Tiffany want to see her?"

Dee had a worried expression. "I think it would help Tiffany if she had someone to help and support her through all of this."

"Do you want me to see if I can find Joyce Hunter?"

"Would you? Thanks."

"You worry too much about other people, Dee." He walked out to his truck and drove away.

* * *

Edna Bristol, Mark Archer, Sara Howard and Mary Harris entered the sheriff's office. Dee stood and picked up the phone, but he had heard them come in and was quickly out of his office. Edna was holding onto her walker. "Jim, can we talk to you?"

"Sure." Realizing that the group would not fit in his office he led the way to the break room. Randy and Dee wandered into the room behind them and stood in the doorway. They were curious what this contingency of citizens wanted.

"What can I help you with?" The Sheriff inquired suspiciously.

"Well," Edna started. "I guess we are here on behalf of Tiffany Hunter. Did you know that terrible mother, Joyce Hunter left town? I don't even think she told Tiffany she was leaving. Mark and the boys have been staying at my house and day before yesterday, she just packed up and left. Didn't say a word to anyone. I don't know how she could do such a thing. That woman is horrible and should never have had children. Anyway, Tiffany doesn't have anyone else in this town to help her." Edna looked around at the others at the table.

Mark spoke up, trying to explain things better. "Sheriff, Edna is not going to press charges about the money and Caroline's death was an accident and not Tiffany's fault so I guess it is only the robbery charge at Kelly's that the DA will prosecute. Is that right?"

"Well, there are a couple of other minor charges." The Sheriff still wasn't sure where this conversation was leading. He felt good after the inquest and thought everyone accepted the decision well. Mark had admitted that Caroline's death was an accident.

"Jim, we want to put in a good word for Tiffany with the DA. How do we go about that?" Mary knew there had to be a way.

"Ahh. Okay. Well, just go explain the circumstances. I would talk to Tiffany's Public Defender too. Her name is Sharon Singleton. I think she's coming to see Tiffany this afternoon." The Sheriff looked at Dee who nodded that the Public Defender had phoned and would be there this afternoon.

"Okay, I'll call Mrs. Singleton and talk to her." Edna was walking better and feeling much more independent.

"If you can set the meeting up for after one, I can be here too," Mary added.

"Sheriff, the boys and I are leaving for Seattle tomorrow. There isn't anything else you need from me is there?" Mark's expression told everyone he was ready to go home.

"No. I think everything has been taken care of. I'm sorry about Caroline and I wish you and the boys the best."

They shook hands and Mark left.

"Meanwhile, who is going to tell Tiffany that her mother left town?" The Sheriff asked, not wanting to be the one.

Edna volunteered, "I know the girl better than anyone else. I need to do it. Mary, want to come with me?"

Mary nodded her consent and stood.

Dee led the ladies back to Tiffany's cell. Tiffany looked up as they entered, her pensive expression made her look older than her nineteen years.

"Hi Tiffany, how are you?" Edna shuffled her walker in and sat on the cot while Mary stood by the cell door.

Being very skeptical of what the women wanted, "Fine."

Tiffany looked at both women closely. She assumed Edna was still angry about the money.

Edna reached over took Tiffany's hand. "Honey, we need to tell you something. Have you heard from you mother?"

Tiffany shook her head to the negative.

"I was afraid of that. Honey, your mother packed her things and left town. She didn't tell anyone where she was going or if she would be back. Mark has been staying at the house and she just packed the other morning and left. She didn't say a thing to him or me. Your things are still there."

Tiffany reached for the tissue box and the tears started. "She said if I ever got in trouble . . .I would be on my own. I guess she meant it."

Dee stepped into the cell area with a cup of mint tea and handed it to Tiffany. "Maybe this will make you feel better." She quickly went back to her office area.

The three women were silent while Tiffany drank her tea.

At last, Tiffany said, "Mom left me. I haven't seen her since the day after the accident. I figured she had packed and left. She wouldn't stay here after what I've done. You would have fired her." Tiffany looked up at Edna.

"I'm doing a lot better now. I should be able to look after myself when I leave rehab this time," Edna explained. "Would you like me to bring some of your things over?"

Mary was watching Tiffany's reaction to the news. She felt the young lady was handling the news as well as could be expected, but she would mention to Dee to keep an eye on her. With everything that was happening, depression was a real concern.

When Tiffany didn't answer Edna, Mary suggested, "You make a list of whatever you need and I'll bring it over, okay?"

Tiffany nodded.

The ladies didn't know what else to do or say. Edna stood and gave the girl a hug. "I'll be back to visit."

Mary gave her a smile and wave as they left.

Tiffany gave a slight nod as she finished her tea. Dee was right she did feel a little better.

\* \* \*

Late that afternoon Sharon Singleton, Tiffany's Public Defender came to visit the prisoner. Dee showed her back to the cell and unlocked the door. Sharon sat down on the cot and set her briefcase on the floor beside her. Tiffany stayed seated in the recliner. She couldn't get up without help.

"Tiffany, how are you doing?" Mrs. Singleton opened her briefcase and took out a paper.

"My foot and leg are broken, I'm sitting in a jail cell, and my mother left town but I guess I'm okay." Her eyes were tearing up.

"Yes, I need to tell you. When I went to look for the money you said was in the book in your dresser; it wasn't there. The book was there but there was no money."

"My mom must have found it." Tiffany was crying so much this last bit of information made her nauseous.

Sharon patted her hand. "Well, this should make you feel better. I've been talking to some of the town's people along with the District Attorney. I can't believe it with all you have done, but several people in Cold Springs want to take care of you."

Tiffany leaned forward in the recliner. "What? I don't know what you are talking about. What do you mean 'they want to take care of me?'"

"I'll explain. This is what the DA, the town people, and I have worked out, if you will agree to it. First, Travis Bristol assured the DA that you borrowed his handgun so the theft of the gun has been dismissed. The Sheriff told the DA he didn't actually see you go off the road so, he can't prove you were driving recklessly. I explained to the DA that you thought the cash from Kelly's was still at your house and you told me to pick it up and give it to him. I explained that your mother may have taken it when she left town." She gave Tiffany a chance to consider this then continued.

"Yes, I'm sure she took it."

"Second, you need to plead guilty to the robbery at Kelly O'Conner's and pay back the remainder of the money you stole. If you are willing to pay the money back, he has agreed to ask the judge to give you six months in the county jail and put you on probation for five years. This is a good deal, Tiffany. I suggest you take it."

Tiffany frowned and thought about it for a minute. "I only have to stay here in jail for six months? I don't have to go to a real prison?"

"That's right. Six months in jail and five years of probation."

"I don't understand. You told me that I could be looking at five years in a woman's prison."

"Well, I met Edna Bristol and two nurses. The rehab lady that used to come to Edna's house, Sarah, I think her name is. Mary Harris the woman who works at the hospital. They all feel that it would be best if you stay here and serve your jail time and they talked the DA into it."

"Why do they want me to stay here? I don't understand." Tiffany was confused. She was trying to figure out what she had done for Edna and the others in the town for them want to help her. She couldn't come up with anything. Her mother had always instilled in her that if you didn't take from people they would take from you. People weren't to be trusted. This whole situation was new and confusing to her. There had only been one other person in her life who had helped her without wanting anything in return, her old high school counselor.

Sharon gave Tiffany a few minutes then asked, "Tiffany, will you agree to plead guilty and accept six months in jail and five years probation?"

"Yes. That is better than I thought I would get." She hesitated. "How will I pay Kelly back if I don't have any money?"

"Kelly doesn't expect to be paid back until you have served your time here and get a job." Tiffany nodded her head in understanding.

"Okay, I will let the county judge know and we can set a date for sentencing. Is there anything I can do for you?"

* * *

Tiffany was sitting in the chair thinking about her future when Dee brought her dinner. "I didn't know what you wanted. The county only pays for the drink and the 'special' at the Wagon Wheel. Tonight the special is pot roast."

Dee set the takeout on the nightstand along with a glass of tea and a fork. "I'm sorry a fork is all we can let you eat with. No knives are allowed in the cells, even plastic ones."

"That's okay, I like their pot roast." The aroma made her hungry, and she remembered that she had a late breakfast before she left the hospital but hadn't had any lunch.

"Do you mind if I sit and talk to you while you eat?"

"No. I would like company."

Dee sat down on the cot. "Tiffany, I've

been doing some checking and if you would like to take some online classes in business, I think I can arrange it. You can borrow my personal laptop computer and the Methodist Church had a fundraiser to help students pay for online courses and you could apply for some of the tuitions. I checked and the college in Gunnison has classes like business law, accounting, finance and office administration. What do you think? Would you be interested in doing something like that?"

Tiffany looked at Dee, the fork halfway to her mouth, "I don't get it. Why does everyone want to help me?"

"Wouldn't you like our help?"

"Yes, but what do you expect from me?" Tiffany sat ramrod straight, a dozen scenarios running through her head. "Do I have to pay you a bunch of money? Work for you without pay? What do you want? Whatever you want, I'm not doing it."

These questions took Dee by surprise. She knew the girl had issues but wasn't sure what they all were. "Tiffany, hasn't anyone ever helped you without expecting anything in return?"

"No! I don't want you to help me. I want you to leave me alone." Her fear of the unknown and being alone overcame all other emotions.

Dee left quietly.

\* \* \*

It took over a month before Mandy and her mother convinced Tiffany that she could accept help from the Methodist Church online college fund and start her classes.

Dee was the Jill-of-all-trades: receptionist, dispatcher, secretary and jail matron. But she would visit with Tiffany when she had extra time. It only took a few weeks for them to become friends. Doctor Levine asked a psychotherapist friend of his from Denver to spend a few hours a day of his fishing vacation talking to Tiffany. This seemed to help and keep her out of the depression she started a week after she was sentenced.

One morning the Sheriff picked up Tiffany's breakfast and took it to her cell. She was in her recliner typing on a computer that sat on a large tray across the arms of the chair. "Good Morning, Tiffany. I brought your breakfast."

Tiffany was very engrossed in what she was doing and didn't look up. "Thanks." She continued typing.

In the reception area, Hobson asked Dee, "Tiffany is certainly into her college courses isn't she?"

"Ah, yes." Dee gave him a sly look out of the corner of her eyes.

"Dee, what is Tiffany typing on that

computer?"

"Well, Sheriff, Tiffany needed some spending money for things that the county doesn't provide so I got her a job typing for the County Commissioners. They really pay quite well, and if she wants to work in an office, she needs to practice her typing. We were able to underbid the lady who used to do it so they gave her the job."

"You underbid poor Mrs. Marsh?"

"'Poor Mrs. Marsh' owns the laundry mart, the dry cleaners and four rental properties. She doesn't need the money. Tiffany does." Dee dismissed the Sheriff and went back to her keyboard.

The End

Thank you for reading my book I hope you enjoyed reading it as much as I enjoyed writing it.

Now, I will ask you to do me a favor, if you like this book please leave a review on Amazon and Goodreads. If you didn't enjoy it, please email me (saracaudell@austin.rr.com) and let me know what you felt the problem was. It is important that I get both positive and negative feedback so I can improve my writing.

If you would like to learn more about the characters and Cold Springs, please visit my website: Saracaudell.com You will see the Wagon
Wheel bar, the town of Cold Springs and more.

If you liked this book you might want to read the first chapter of Cold Springs Sanctuary, in the next page.

I have three other books now on Kobo, Nook, iBooks and Amazon
They Don't Shoot Horses
Wild Revelations
Shattered Sanctuary

Again, thank you for purchasing and reading my book.

Sara

## About the Author

Sara Caudell grew up in a small ranching community in Colorado where she learned to judge beef on the hoof and under plastic wrap. After moving around the country for her husband's career and catching college courses as she could, she finally found herself in one place long enough to finish her degree. She was an artist, raised three children, managed offices, and started her own business before weaving her stories and experiences into novels. She now lives in central Texas with her patient husband and four cats. In her spare time she does genealogy research and nurses orphan kittens and injured cats for the local animal shelter.

*Cold Springs Sanctuary*

*No good deed goes unpunished.*

In a remote Colorado ranching community, a
horse trainer and a rancher provide women with
sanctuary. All is well -- until the center for abused
women headquartered in Texas is burglarized and
a powerful legislator starts looking for his
wayward daughter. But this is only the beginning
of the problems.

# CHAPTER 1

## Kerrville, Texas:

"Hello." Dale Rittenhouse answered his cell phone and listened intently. A frown covered his broad, suntanned face. His end of the conversation was "Uh-huh. Uh-huh. Okay. Thanks, J. R." Amanda, his daughter, sitting across the table at their favorite restaurant, knew there was a major problem. Their ranch manager never bothered her father for anything except dire emergencies.

Dale hung up as anguish played across his face. "There's been a break-in at the house. We need to finish eating and get back home. There was a lot of damage in your office. J. R. thinks computer equipment is missing. The Sheriff is on his way there." Her father's attention went to his plate of steak and a baked potato.

Fear clutched Amanda's stomach. "Should we get this to-go?" Amanda pointed at her trout dinner.

"No, just eat fast." Dale saw the worry on Amanda's face as she hurriedly wolfed down part of her dinner.

"Dad, do you think . . ."

"Don't worry about that 'til we know more."

They finished eating, paid and hurried to their black SUV. Slow panic and dread reflected in Amanda's face as they headed back to the ranch in silence.

Looking over at his daughter, Dale couldn't see her face. With her head down, her long brown hair hid her profile. Unconsciously her thumbnail scrapped at her nail polish, slowly demolished her new manicure. He knew her thoughts; they were the same fears nagging his mind. He gripped the steering wheel tighter and sighed.

Dale had started the Women's Underground, for battered women, after his drunk, abusive brother-in-law (now on death-row) shot Dale's wife and her sister. The killings were a tragic awakening for Dale and Amanda. Dale wanted to stop the killing of other women by a boyfriend or spouse. He hoped this would alleviate his guilt for not recognizing the prospective violence in his own family.

After researching women's shelter organizations in large cities, he realized their business model would not work in rural areas. Close-knit communities didn't air their dirty laundry in public. The shelters had to be more discreet. They could not be openly advertised; the locations would be kept secret. Brochures at public gatherings and word of mouth would convey their existence. The contact would be a 1-800 number.

The other problem Dale saw with large shelters was the lack of communication with the women after they left the shelter. He wanted better follow-up and support. Recidivism was high with abused women; he wanted to make sure the dependency was broken.

Five years ago Dale funded the first location and got it up and running, then he used his political influence to help fund the others. The non-profit's goal was simple: help women get away from the abuser, give them temporary refuge, counseling, and permanent placement as far from the abuser as practical. Amanda had taken over as administrator of the Underground when Dale was re-elected County Commissioner, two years ago.

The large limestone gate announcing the entrance to the Rittenhouse ranch shined in the headlights before Amanda voiced her fear, "Dad, do you think someone found out? Do you think they were after the records?"

"Let's not panic 'til we find out more." Dale always assessed the facts before putting forth an opinion. The records being stolen was his first thought too, but he hoped the burglars were after valuables, not information.

Arriving at the large ranch-style house, Dale pulled the Tahoe into the driveway beside the sheriff's cruiser. Amanda and Dale emerged from the car, hurried through the front door and down the hall to her back office. Amanda felt her father's hands on her shoulders stopping her in the doorway. They stared at the damage as a deputy scurried around taking photos. Someone had swept everything off the top of her desk onto the floor. The receipt files, notepaper, paperclips, pens, and folders were strewn across the rug between the door and her desk. Most of the files on the computer consisted of ranch accounting, cattle records, ranch mail and Dale's correspondence. She surveyed the room and saw that her computer, an external hard-drive and a large CD case were missing.

The separate hard drive held the records of the Women's Underground. Part of the information was coded, but the final placements had actual street and city addresses. Amanda's eyes went to the crack behind her desk where a stapler had hit the wall. The horse photos from her wall were on the floor with broken glass and frames. The overturned chairs were by the cracked window behind her desk.

After the deputy finished taking photographs and lifting fingerprints he allowed the Rittenhouses into the room. Amanda, shaken but concentrating on the scene, gave them a list of the missing equipment. She even rummaged through her files and found serial numbers. The Sheriff started speculating whether the burglar was after something specific on the computers or wanted the computers to sell for pocket money. Then, assessing the mess, he commented, "I think whoever did this needs a course in anger management."

The remark didn't sit well with Dale. The Sheriff had just made the break-in personal, not random. He glanced at Amanda who took a deep breath but didn't flinch.

"Dale, is there county information stored on the computer that someone would want bad enough to break in and steal it?"

"Can't think of any. Once in a while I'll send a note to another commissioner or a constituent. Just routine reminders. Stuff like that. Nothin' to do with county contracts or bids." Dale wasn't much of a keyboarder and anything along those lines, if he could delegate it to the commission secretary, he did.

"Don't have any ranch secrets someone would want?" the Sheriff gave a half laugh, but stared at Dale. Amanda's eyes widened. The two deputies taking photos and fingerprints listened with interest.

"Can I talk to you outside, Sheriff?"

Dale led the Sheriff down the hall and out through the patio doors in the den. They passed J. R. sitting in one of the overstuffed chairs playing nervously with his hat. Standing on the patio and taking a deep breath, Dale said. "The hard drive held the Underground's records."

"I was wandering." The Sheriff Scott took off his hat and scratched his head. "You think that's what they were after?"

The worried frown on Dale's face answered his question. The Sheriff had been advised of the Underground when it first started and had referred three women to it over the years. He had also spread the 1-800 number around to other rural law enforcement officers. "I'll look for the hard-drive first thing tomorrow, Dale. I'll have the pawnshops and computer geeks checked out first thing in the morning. If it's okay, I'll suggest to my men that the equipment contains confidential county information on it? That'd give it a sense of importance without mentioning the Underground."

Dale nodded, no less worried, but still grateful. "Sounds good, thanks, Sheriff. Let me know when you find anything."

Dale went back to Amanda's office, J. R. left with a nod of his head and the Sheriff met his men at their cars. The Sheriff and his deputies were driving away when Amanda turned to her father.

"Did you tell the Sheriff?"

"Yes. He'll tell them the computer and hard-drive have county information on them. First thing tomorrow I will go to town and buy a new computer. You send the attorney a back-up of all the records, don't you?"

Amanda nodded trying to follow her father's train of thought.

"Call him first thing in the morning and get a copy, go through it and see if anything relevant jumps out. How many people in this county know about the Underground?"

Amanda paused for a minute. "Besides you, me, the Sheriff and the attorney . . . maybe two . . . three. The entire organization only has seven people on the payroll, just the women who run the safe houses."

"How about volunteers?"

"We have eleven full time volunteers, and the doctors and psychologists all work on a contract basis. The problem is the addresses of the safe houses were on the payroll records. Most expenses and other information pass through the attorneys in Ft. Worth. I'm hoping who ever took the equipment needed money, like the Sheriff suggested." She tried to be logical. After all they had taken the petty cash box with about two hundred dollars in it. "We've gone through so much to keep any evidence of the Underground away from the ranch," Amanda lamented.

"You're probably right. Just a need for money," he let out a sigh. "However, let the directors of the safe houses know what's happened. Tell them not to panic. Keep accepting women. Business as usual. I'll do a phone conference with John and the others directors tomorrow morning."

Still worrying, they retired to their bedrooms. Dale took care of funding for the Underground. Amanda was the one who screened the women's information and set up the contacts, the safe houses and the transportation arrangements. Trying to assess what information could be retrieved from the scattered and coded records, Amanda finally got up and went down stairs for a glass of wine. It was after one in the morning before she returned to her bed and fell asleep.

Meanwhile, Dale sat on the bed making notes for the directors meeting. He knew he would have to discuss the worst-case scenario: an angry, abusive husband going after his wife. And worse still there was always the possibility of the burglar selling the remaining information to other abusive husbands. The thought of hot headed, violent men looking for and finding their wives sent shivers of fear and regret through his body. He would have to come up with his own plan to catch the thief. Least worst problem: the public knowing he, Amanda and the ranch ran the Women's Underground.

They would have visitors, abused women seeking shelter and dangerous husbands looking for missing wives. The ranch didn't have the security for that. He doubted if the ranch could even be made secure for such visitors. The Underground taking over his life and family ranch was not an option. He would pull the plug on it before he would live with it on his doorstep. If it came to that, he could always help raise money for a shelter in Houston or San Antonio. He had a contingency plan for later. Now he had to deal with the immediate problem. Dale lay back on the bed remembering his murdered wife and the best years of his life with the only woman he had ever loved.

Made in the USA
Coppell, TX
24 April 2020

22219273R00164